The Dawson Pond Murders

A JOHN WESLEY O'TOOLE NOVEL

ALSO BY WILLIAM RAWLINGS

The Garden of Earthly Delights (2024)
(A John Wesley O'Toole Novel)

Crypto (2023)
(A John Wesley O'Toole Novel)

The Columbus Stocking Strangler (2022)

Lighthouses of the Georgia Coast (2021)

Six Inches Deeper (2020)

The Girl with Kaleidoscope Eyes (2019)
(A John Wesley O'Toole Novel)

The Strange Journey of the Confederate Constitution (2017)

The Second Coming of the Invisible Empire (2016)

A Killing on Ring Jaw Bluff (2013)

The Dawson Pond Murders

A JOHN WESLEY O'TOOLE NOVEL

William Rawlings

MERCER UNIVERSITY PRESS
Macon, Georgia

MUP/ P725

Published by Mercer University Press
1501 Mercer University Drive
Macon, Georgia 31207

29 28 27 26 25 5 4 3 2 1

Books published by Mercer University Press are printed on acid-free paper that meets the requirements of the American National Standard for Information Sciences—Permanence of Paper for Printed Library Materials.

Printed and bound in the United States.

This book is set in Adobe Garamond Pro.

Cover/jacket design by Burt&Burt.

ISBN 978-0-88146-986-8
Cataloging-in-Publication Data is available from the Library of Congress

AUTHOR'S FOREWORD

Sometimes the best of intentions can lead to the worst of outcomes. When John Wesley O'Toole decides to ask Jenna, his would-be fiancée, to allow him to take her young son, Robert, fishing, he hopes it will strengthen their relationship and help lead to her giving her hand in marriage. O'Toole, a disbarred attorney-turned art dealer, seeks to return both his and Jenna's lives to some sort of normalcy. Instead, the horrid discovery that had lain hidden for years below the waters of the Dawson pond will shatter both of their worlds.

This is the fourth in the John Wesley O'Toole mystery series, following *The Girl with Kaleidoscope Eyes*, *Crypto*, and *The Garden of Earthly Delights*. Like all works in this series, *The Dawson Pond Murders* is written as a stand-alone novel. Though I am certain fans of mystery and suspense will enjoy them, it is not necessary to have read others in this series to appreciate this tale. John O'Toole is a fascinating, if imperfect, character, seemingly tracked by misfortune, but whose struggles and adventures have become a favorite of many readers.

MERCER UNIVERSITY PRESS

Endowed by

TOM WATSON BROWN
and
THE WATSON-BROWN FOUNDATION, INC.

The Dawson Pond Murders

CHAPTER 1

The "pond," as Mr. Dawson called it, was down a barely visible dirt track winding its way through a forest of pine and hardwood on "the family farm," another of his terms. I was driving his twenty-year-old Chevy S-10 pickup while his grandson, Robert, somewhere between age nine and ten, sat next to me, excited to be going fishing for the first time in his short life. Mr. Dawson had insisted that I take the pickup, observing that my car would be unlikely to make it. "Probably get stuck. I don't want to have to come down there and pull y'all out," he observed.

At the bottom of a slight slope, the woods gave way to what at one time must have been a modest-sized pasture, now periodically mowed to provide an open space next to a small spring-fed lake, about three acres in size at most. "There's some big bass in there, and some bream, too, if the bass ain't eat 'em all up. And if you'll look over next to the dam, you'll see a flat-bottom boat turned upside down and chained to an oak tree. Paddles are up under it, and the key to the lock on the chain is on a nail kinda high up on the backside of the oak. Or y'all can fish from the bank if you want." Mr. Dawson was explicit in his instructions. "If you gonna use worms, they got them at that little convenience store you're gonna see on the righthand side of the road on the way out there." He paused a moment, then, "But if you gonna use that spinning rod you done spent money on, I'd use a Rooster Tail, one with a big treble hook. Reel it in real slow-like. Let it sink down a bit and then give it a jerk. Drives them bass crazy."

I had purchased two new cane poles and a not-especially-expensive spinning rod, just in case. The goal was to introduce Robert to fishing, and maybe get to know him better, primarily because I was in love with his mother, whom I planned to ask to marry me when the time was right. We stopped on the way at the convenience store and bought a small container of fishing worms. I planned to try out the spinning rod while Robert worked with the pole. He was a small-framed, somewhat shy boy, still a child but very much eager to pursue the trappings of manhood, one of which was fishing, he informed me. "I don't see my dad much at all, but maybe you know that," he said, sounding as if he were revealing a dark secret. "He lives in Savannah."

"I do, but I understand. Your mother is so proud of you, and that's important."

"But the other kids' dads…," he began, stopping without finishing the sentence.

"I know, but let's get things ready to catch some fish," I said as I parked the pickup. Robert grinned.

I thought we'd try fishing from the bank first. I wanted to show Robert the basics of rigging his pole, baiting a hook, adjusting the plastic float, and launching the line into the water without getting it hung on anything. He caught on quickly, casting the bait out into the pond with ease. No more than two minutes passed before the bobber trembled, lurched away from the shore and disappeared under the water. "Okay!" I yelled. "He's running with the bait. Now give him a quick jerk of the pole." Robert complied as if he had been doing this all of his life. Within two minutes, we were looking at a large red-breasted bream dangling from his line. I helped him remove it from the hook and put it on a stringer as Robert rebaited his line, insisting that he needed no help.

Casually allowing him to continue trying to do things on

his own, I moved down the bank a few yards and, using the spinning rod, began casting a lure into the depths of the pond, slowly reeling it in per the instructions of Mr. Dawson. Within twenty minutes, Robert had caught two more bream, while I had not had a single strike at my lure. As he put the third fish on the stringer, he turned to me and said, "Mr. John, will you show me how to use that kind of pole you're fishing with?"

"Sure," I replied, pleased at his eagerness. "It's really a completely different way to catch fish. So let me show you...," I continued, explaining each step as I cast and reeled in the lure several times. Robert watched and listened intently as I pointed out the details of using a rod and reel.

"I want to try it," he said. I smiled and handed him the rod. I had anticipated that he might want to use it, so I had strung it with twenty-five-pound-test line, unlikely to break and lose the lure in case he got snagged on some underwater object. Again, I went over how to reel and jerk the lure to attract bass. By the fifth or sixth try, Robert had the casting part down, after which we worked for a few more minutes on reeling the line in. I wanted him to take the initiative and learn from his own mistakes, so I said I'd sit on the tailgate of the pickup and watch him from a distance while he fished. In truth, I was a little afraid he might snag me with the lure as he was attempting to cast, but didn't mention that. I suggested that he move over about fifty feet, casting into the deeper water near the dam and trying his luck there.

Robert appeared eager and determined to show me what he could do. After a dozen or more casts, he seemed to be getting the hang of the process, displaying remarkable success in spite of his age, size and lack of previous experience. After about ten minutes, he appeared to have a strike on his line. He yelled "Look!" and attempted to set the hook with a firm jerk on the rod. His line was briefly taut, then went slack as the presumed fish on the other end got away.

Obviously excited, he yelled, "Tell me what I should do next time."

"Maybe give the fish a little more time before you try to set the hook. Try reeling it in a bit slower." He was trying so hard. I was proud of him.

Again, Robert cast in the same general area, this time pulling in the lure more slowly, allowing it to sink nearly to the bottom as he reeled. Suddenly his line grew taut again. He waited a few seconds before giving the rod a sharp jerk, hoping to set the hook. If he had hooked a large fish, the tension on the line should have tightened. Instead, it sagged once he stopped reeling for a moment. He turned to me with a puzzled look. "I think you may have gotten snagged on something." His expression turned to disappointment. "That's okay, and in some ways that's good. Everybody that fishes gets snagged once in a while. This will give me a chance to show you what to do."

Walking over, I took the rod from Robert and, locking the reel, pulled gently on the line. It did not move, suggesting he was hooked into a solid object of some sort. I moved a few feet away from the edge of the pond, and pointing the rod in the direction of the line, pulled directly so as to put the force on the reel, not the breakable rod. Nothing happened; the line refused to move. I backed up a bit and gave it a slight jerk, then another using more force. No change. Turning to Robert, I said, "Looks like we may have to break the line. If we do, that's okay. Happens all the time."

"I'm so sorry," Robert said, looking like he might burst out in tears, "I didn't mean to…."

"Hey, it's okay. This is part of the sport, like golf, maybe, where your ball ends up in a water hazard." I wasn't sure he understood the analogy, but he seemed to relax.

I gave the rod another firm jerk, and this time it moved. I tried tightening the line on the reel. It moved slowly, with evident resistance. "Is it loose?" Robert asked.

"Yeah, I think so. It's moving and it looks like we're dragging in something hooked on the end. It's probably an old limb or something like that. Maybe we'll be able to get the lure back after all." Robert now smiled.

I continued to slowly reel in whatever was hung on the line. As I dragged it into the shallow water nearer the shore, I could make out an oblong mud-covered object, not likely to break the heavy line. Probably a small log. Pulling it on the edge of the bank, I stooped down to try to unhook the lure, which appeared to be caught on one end of the object. It was then I realized that rather than a piece of wood, it was a shoe, a muck-covered, tightly-laced tennis shoe encrusted with scum from the pond's bottom. The treble hook of the lure had snagged the top of the back of the foot opening, sinking two barbs into the fabric. I wanted to try to extract the hook without destroying it, so I reached out and swished the object in the water to remove some of the debris covering it. I noticed it seemed somewhat heavy, but presumed it was filled with mud. As I moved it back and forth in the shallow water, I noticed something inside the shoe. I fished out more of the muck with my finger and swished it once again. When I examined the shoe more closely this time I realized, to my horror, that the material inside the shoe was not mud or muck. It appeared to be a bone.

CHAPTER 2

Two weeks earlier:

It was one of those rare times when most things in my life appeared to be going smoothly. The art gallery was thriving; sales were steady and substantial. The dark days of the past were rapidly fading into distant memories: the two years I served in prison for vehicular homicide, the loss of my law license and with it my career, and perhaps most importantly, the implosion of my marriage and the loss of contact with my children. The one constant bright spot in my daily existence was Jenna. Like me, she too had a dark history, a struggling divorcée who gradually slipped into the shadowy world of drugs, and all that came with it. We met by chance at a court-mandated substance-abuse aftercare session, cautiously beginning a relationship that had now lasted more than two years. As I labored to forge my new career as a gallery owner and art dealer, Jenna strove to regain her place in the world, providing love and support and guidance to her young son, Robert, the product of her own failed marriage. They lived in a modest apartment in her hometown of Claxton, a small community about an hour's drive inland from Savannah.

I wanted to marry Jenna. There was no doubt in my mind about that. I was convinced that the union would do much toward making both of our lives complete. We had discussed it, not in great detail, but enough for me to be certain that Jenna felt the same way. Yet, for a myriad of reasons, both voiced and held in silence, she seemed reluctant to take this huge leap of faith. Although she never spoke of it, the emotional trauma of her past failures seemed to weigh heavily on every potentially life-changing decision. She still carried her ex-husband's name, McClure, explaining that she didn't "want the kids at Robert's school to ask why his mother had a different last name." I had to respect her caution.

One afternoon, as I was at the gallery in the middle of some mindless task, it suddenly occurred to me that I was on the wrong path. While I had been focusing on building a life together, I had been blindly and foolishly fixated solely on my relationship with Jenna. If we were to marry, with a few short words of committal I would become not only a husband, but a stepfather and a son-in-law, a member of a family I hardly knew, with new responsibilities and obligations. In that brief moment of revelation, I realized I needed to broaden my thinking and plans to include Jenna's son, Robert, and her parents, the Dawsons. I knew them, of course, but only in the role of Jenna's friend and possible suitor, not as a future husband and member of the family.

I felt especially sorry for Robert. The more I thought about it, I realized that in some ways his situation was similar to mine, growing up in a "broken home" as my grandmother described it. I was an only child, the product of my mother's first marriage and a casualty of the several that followed. My parents separated when I was young, eventually going through a bitter divorce. Five other marriages followed, the last of which ended with my mother's death from a combination of alcohol and drugs. As a child and later as a teenager, I was bounced back and forth, spending most of the time with my grandparents in Savannah. My grandfather, a physician, became my role model and surrogate father figure during those turbulent years. I came to love and admire him as the parent I never knew. I fondly remembered the many Saturdays we spent fishing in the coastal marshes near Savannah. I'd talk and he would listen, sharing his thoughts and dispensing wisdom to an insecure man-child. Privately, I credited him for whatever success in life I had achieved before my world fell apart.

If I hoped to marry Jenna, I had to include Robert in my plans. And I would seek to become a stable figure in Robert's life, as my grandfather had in mine. As a first step, I would see if he would like for me to take him fishing.

I gently broached the idea to Jenna as we sat eating a late lunch at Claxton's Huddle House, located next to the community's only shopping mall, a struggling strip center on a stretch of four-lane highway just north of town. "Really?" she said, looking surprised. "You've never mentioned that before."

"I know, but I've been thinking. When I was that age my grandfather would take me out fishing in the marshes. We'd have fun, but more importantly we'd talk…."

"About what?" Jenna interrupted, now sounding either curious or suspicious. I couldn't tell which.

"Nothing special, just whatever came to mind, really. I know Robert spends a lot of time around your father, but he's a lot older and kind of an authority figure. I thought maybe he might want to talk to someone he could feel more relaxed with, maybe ask questions, or advice, or whatever."

Jenna pursed her lips, "Gosh, John, he's not even ten years old yet. What in the world…?"

"When I was that age, I had a lot of things I wanted to talk about, a lot of questions I wanted answered. My granddad was always there for me, ready to answer or explain, or help me figure things out. He was always very neutral, non-judgmental. Always ready to give advice, especially about things I was embarrassed or afraid to discuss with my mother."

She was silent, laying down her fork and lost in thought as she stared out the window. Then, "I guess my little boy is growing up. And I realize sometimes I'm too close to the situation to see the changes as they take place." She paused, then looked at me with a gentle smile. "Yes, I think that would be a great idea, and I know Robert would enjoy it. You have become so much a part of my life, and I think it would be a wonderful idea for you to become part of his."

I reached across the table and squeezed her hand, grinning.

CHAPTER 3

When I first suggested the idea, Robert appeared ecstatic at the thought of going fishing, peppering me with questions about what he should wear, or if he should worry about snakes or alligators, or hooking fish so large that they might break his line. I assured him that nothing like that would happen, explaining as best I knew how that this would just be a fun and relaxing afternoon, a chance for him to learn the basics of fishing and for us to get to know each other better. Now, he sat glumly on the tailgate of the pickup as we waited for the sheriff to arrive. "What did you find in that old shoe that made you call the police?" he asked for what seemed like the tenth time.

"To be honest, Robert, I'm not really sure," I lied, "but it was something that I thought might be important, like maybe the shoe belonged to someone who was missing."

"What do you mean by 'missing?'" he asked, reminding me through his naivety that he was still a child.

"Let's just wait and see what the sheriff says." I hoped that would satisfy his curiosity for the time being. It seemed obvious to me that the tennis shoe was full of bones that appeared to be human, strongly suggesting that it was once attached to the leg of a body whose remains now lay in the depths of the lake. Assuming my assessment was correct, it was unlikely that anything positive could result from this discovery.

The first thing I did after realizing what I had discovered was call Jenna on my cell phone. I didn't go into detail but explained that we might be a bit late getting back to her apartment. I thought it would be best to have someone from law enforcement confirm my suspicions, then take Robert home so I could explain things to her in person, face-to-face. Any attempt to do so over the phone would have been disastrous. Jenna seemed somewhat suspicious, but accepted my explanation. I then dialed 911, briefly described what I had found to the operator and asked her to send out someone from the sheriff's office. She called back in less than five minutes to tell me that a patrol car and two officers were on the way and should arrive within the next twenty minutes. I asked Robert to watch the truck while I jogged the quarter mile or so back to the road where I unlocked the gate and left it open for the sheriff's officers.

I had scarcely gotten back to the lake when an Evans County sheriff's deputy vehicle, formerly white but now splashed with mud, negotiated its way down the narrow forest track. Two officers emerged, cautiously eyeing the surroundings before approaching Robert and me as we stood next to Mr. Dawson's pickup. They introduced themselves as Sergeants Gordon and Eason. "Someone reported finding a tennis shoe with a bone in it—maybe a human bone. Are you Mr. O'Toole?" Eason asked. I told him I was, and in the same sentence instructed Robert to go over and sit on the flat-bottomed boat chained to the oak tree. He did not need to hear the conversation that was sure to follow.

I spent the next ten minutes trying to explain to the deputies the sequence of events that led to the 911 call. They appeared somewhat skeptical until I showed them the shoe and the apparent bones seen inside of it. The patrol car's driver headed back to the vehicle to contact the sheriff and ask for backup. "So do you own this property?" the other deputy asked.

"No, it belongs to my girlfriend's family. The boy over there is her son. I was taking him fishing, but you see how that turned out...."

"Have you contacted her or anyone else?"

"Yes, I called her about the same time I called 911. I didn't go over the details because, well...." At that point we were interrupted by what appeared to be Jenna's car rapidly bouncing down the muddy lane toward the lake. She parked just behind the deputies' vehicle and, seeing Robert sitting forlornly on the boat near the dam, bounded over to see if he was all right. The deputies and I stared in silence. "I guess that's the kid's mother, right?" Sgt. Gordon asked.

"Yes," I replied, trying to read Jenna's body language.

"She looks pretty unhappy to me," Gordon observed.

"Can't really blame her," Eason said.

By this time Jenna was headed back to where we stood, Robert's hand gripped tightly in hers. She appeared angry, an assessment confirmed by her voice. "What is this Robert's telling me about finding someone's bone in a shoe that he caught on his hook? I'm not sure I'm hearing him right—it doesn't seem to make sense."

"Jenna, I didn't want to upset you. Robert's hook got snagged on something. We reeled it in to get the lure unhooked and it turned out to be a tennis shoe. I saw something inside of it that worried me, so before I did anything else I thought I should notify the sheriff and let someone confirm what I'd found. I called you first, though, and...."

"Why didn't you tell me all this first?" Jenna's eyes narrowed as she spoke. "This is my son you are with—a person you are responsible for. Don't you think that's the most important thing? What do you think something like this will do...." She stopped suddenly in mid-sentence, announcing, "We're going home now," and dragged Robert, his hand still clenched tightly in hers, toward her car.

I yelled out, "I'll call you as soon as I can." Jenna

pretended not to hear. Strapping Robert into the front passenger seat, she threw her car in reverse, backed up and turned around, her tires spewing fountains of mud in our direction as she left.

"I think she's more than a little pissed off," one of the deputies said.

"Yep," the other replied.

"I'm really sorry about that. I didn't tell her the whole story when I called her, and...."

"Don't worry about it. I didn't get a chance to tell you that the sheriff said he was on his way," Sgt. Eason said, glancing at his watch. "Should be here pretty much any time now."

For the next ten minutes or so, the deputies interviewed me, taking notes regarding the details of discovering the tennis shoe. "So you've never been here before, you said?"

"No, I wanted to get to know Jenna's son better because, just maybe, sometime before too long I want to ask her to marry me. And...."

"Good luck there," Sgt. Gordon interrupted.

"...And this little lake seemed like a good option. Actually, Jenna's father suggested it. I don't know the details at all, but it's been in their family for a long time."

"Do you have any idea who has access to this property?"

"No, like I said, this is my first time here and I don't know any of the details. I know they keep the gate locked and there's a "No Trespassing" sign up by the road...."

"Did Jenna's father—what did you say his name was? Dawson, right? Did he give you a key?"

"No, there's a heavy chain and lock on the gate, but it's a combination lock. You need a four-digit number to open it."

"I guess you don't have any idea who might have that combination...?" We were interrupted by another Evans

County sheriff's car approaching. "Okay, looks like the boss is here."

The Evans County Sheriff, a heavy-set man in his early forties, extracted himself from the patrol car and ambled over to where we stood by Mr. Dawson's pickup. He nodded at the deputies and stuck out his hand to shake mine. "I'm Peter Hearn," he said, not feeling it necessary to add that he was the county sheriff. "Sergeants Eason and Gordon say you think you may have found some bones in a shoe. Is that right?" Once again I explained the sequence of events that led to the discovery of the tennis shoe, a once-white Nike brand with a blue swoosh logo emblazoned on each side, now stained a deep brown by pond water and mud. I held it out for his inspection.

"I hate to say it, Mr. O'Toole, but I agree with you," Hearn said after examining the shoe in detail. "It's laced up pretty tight, so it's not like someone took the shoe off and threw it in the pond. And I'm not an expert, but that sure looks like a bunch of bones down inside of it. And assuming there ain't no apes or monkeys walking around with Nike shoes on, we gotta assume there's something going on here." Turning to the deputies, he continued, "We need to get someone down here to guard the property and make sure no one touches anything until we can get a team in to investigate. I'll make some calls and see if we can round up some scuba divers. I believe the first thing to do is see what else is down on the bottom of that pond."

Turning to me, Sheriff Hearn continued, "Now we need to get you back at headquarters and take a formal statement from you, Mr. O'Toole. And of course we'll need to interview the owners of the property, and find out who has been out here. We're going to need the crime lab to look at that," he pointed at the tennis shoe, "and if the divers find something more, there's a good chance we're going to need to drain the pond. Lots to do, so let's get started." He paused, turned and looked directly at me. "And I understand you live in Savannah, so you'll need to stay in close touch."

If I had set out with plans to ruin my relationship with Jenna, her son, and her parents, I could not have done a better job.

CHAPTER 4

Sheriff Hearn asked Sgt. Gordon to stay at the scene, while Sgt. Eason accompanied him back to the sheriff's office, located just behind the Evans County Courthouse in what passed for Claxton's downtown. He asked me to meet him there in a couple of hours. Gordon strolled about inspecting the area while I sat in the pickup and tried to call Jenna. The call went directly to voicemail. I waited five minutes and tried again. Still no answer. I texted her a longish note saying I was sorry, that I didn't mean for events to work out as they did, and that I loved both her and Robert. No reply. She was obviously upset, and probably quite angry at the way she perceived I had handled the situation.

Feeling somewhat desperate, I waited about fifteen minutes and called the landline of the Dawsons, Jenna's parents. Mrs. Dawson answered with a neutral "Hello," followed by silence. I could hear some commotion in the background, a jumble of voices and what sounded like Robert crying. "Mrs. Dawson, this is John...," I began.

"I know who it is, Mr. O'Toole. I recognized your number." Her voice was icy.

"I wanted to call and let you know what happened, what was going on...."

"You're a little late. Sheriff Hearn is here now and going over things with us. And that hollering you hear, that's Robert. He's scared and upset. We're trying to calm things down."

"Is Jenna there?"

"Yes, but she doesn't want to talk with you just now," Mrs. Dawson said. Then in a lower voice scarcely above a whisper, "I kinda think you're getting blamed for things you didn't do, so give it a while and call her back, maybe tomorrow. I'll tell her you called and...."

At that point I heard Mr. Dawson yell out. "If that's O'Toole, tell him I said he can bring my pickup back on Monday. We'll keep an eye on his car."

Still in a low voice, Mrs. Dawson asked, "Did you hear that? Jenna will be at work and we can talk. The sheriff says he's planning on meeting you a bit later this afternoon at his office. Giving everyone a couple of days to cool off while we try to figure out what's going on seems to be the best thing at the moment." I thanked her and hung up. I got the impression that they were not angry with me but rather were dealing with Jenna's reaction to the situation.

I spoke with Deputy Gordon, gave him the combination to the lock on the roadside gate, and drove back to town to meet with the sheriff. The deputy said one of the officers would be at the pond around the clock until it was determined whether a crime had been committed, or if this was something else, maybe a trespasser who sneaked in to fish in the pond and accidently drowned. I tossed the possibilities back and forth in my mind as I drove. The Dawson farm was located in a sparsely populated area of slightly rolling hills of open farmland and timber in the northern part of the county, perhaps five or six miles in a direct line south of Interstate 16, the main transportation corridor between the Georgia coast and the metropolis of Atlanta. I didn't know the details, including the total area of the tract, or how long they had owned it.

The sheriff had arrived back at his office a few minutes before I got there. I was shown into a small windowless interview room and told to wait. I sat in an uncomfortable straight-backed wooden chair as two cameras peered down on me from opposite walls. After about fifteen minutes, Sheriff Hearn and

Sgt. Eason entered and sat down in two equally uncomfortable chairs across the table from me. Hearn was holding a sheaf of papers in his hand. "Well, Mr. O'Toole, we really do appreciate you calling us about this shoe you found. I took the liberty of running a quick background check on you and see that you seem to be very familiar with the criminal justice system, and from both sides it would appear."

I did not react, displaying only a slight smile. "That's correct, but that has nothing to do with why I called 911 today."

Hearn smiled back, "Didn't say it did, now. Just want to establish were we stand." Looking at the papers in front of him, he continued, "It says here you were an attorney at one time, and did two years of hard time in Reidsville for...," he glanced at a printout in his hand, "...here it is, vehicular homicide."

"That's correct." I continued to smile calmly, realizing Hearn was trying to see how I would react, gauging my reliability as a witness. "But I own an art gallery in Savannah now. That's how I make a living."

"So, I know you gave a statement to my deputies earlier, but if our suspicions—and by that I mean both mine and yours—turn out to be correct, this could well be a case of the wrongful death of whoever owned that shoe. If you wouldn't mind, let's start at the top and go over the whole series of events. And just to be sure we don't miss anything, we'll be recording this." Hearn laid a small digital recorder on the table and pressed a button. A red light flashed on.

For the next few minutes, I went over the details of the day, explaining I wanted to take my girlfriend's son fishing, that it was her father's suggestion that we try the small lake on their farm and so on, up to the tennis shoe being snagged on the hook of Robert's lure. Eason listened intently; Hearn jotted down an occasional note. "You said you'd never been there before, is that correct?" I nodded. "And it was Mr. Dawson's suggestion that you fish there?"

"Yes. He's very fond of his grandson and appeared to be happy that I was taking him fishing. It's a small lake, private, and a good place to learn the basics when he's just starting out."

"I see," Hearn said. "All that makes perfect sense. We have a big job ahead of us though, a lot of which will depend on what the divers find." He paused, "I guess I didn't tell you, I have a crew of fellows that do volunteer underwater searches for law enforcement. They'll be there Monday morning about nine o'clock. If you're available, I'd appreciate your being there to show them exactly where to start the search."

"I'll be there," I said, thinking I needed to come to Claxton anyway to bring back the pickup and retrieve my car.

Hearn stuffed the sheaf of papers in a folder, giving me the impression that the interview was over. Then, folding his arms over his chest, he asked, "Tell me about your relationship with Ms. McClure."

I frowned. "Why? What does she have to do with this?"

"As far as I know, nothing. But as I'm sure you recognize from your past experience with law enforcement, you never know what sort of things are going to crop up. She grew up here, you know, and this is a small town. In some sense of the word, we're all neighbors. Since I'm the sheriff, I hear all sorts of things—good things, as well as bad things, mind you—about the folks who are fortunate enough to call Evans County home. I would guess you know at least some things about Jenna's past. Now, I'm not talking about the Dawsons, they are fine people, but she went off to school and got married and divorced and started running with the wrong crowd. Got into drugs pretty bad at one time I hear, working at that—what do they call it?—'gentleman's club' in Savannah. She had her share of run-ins with the law, too, all of which we can pull up on the computer with the click of a few buttons. I just love modern technology, don't you?" Hearn paused, grinning for a moment, waiting for his words to sink in. "You don't suppose that some of her associates—I'm sorry, former associates—might have had a hand in things that might have happened at the Dawson pond?"

Hearn's use of the term "might have" annoyed me. "Sheriff, you know my past. You know Jenna's past. I'll bet there are a lot of people in this fine community who did things or got involved with people or into situations they later regretted. I know Jenna. I can promise you from the depths of my soul, if you find some criminal activity that's connected to that shoe we found, Jenna had nothing to do with it. She's changed. She's a mother who loves her son and is trying to do the right thing for him and his future."

"I hope you're right, Mr. O'Toole. I don't mean to insult you or Jenna or either of y'all's reputations. It's just my job to be naturally suspicious."

"It's okay, I…," I began.

"But one thing," Hearn interrupted. "Why was she so upset about what happened today? Her son really wasn't exposed to anything, and he probably wouldn't have understood it if he had been. Was she worried about what was found?"

The sheriff stared at me, waiting for my reply. I didn't know what to say.

CHAPTER 5

The sheriff's vague hints about Jenna's possible involvement with the discovery on her family's property infuriated me. My overtly calm reaction required conscious restraint. There was something deep inside my psyche that made me want to leap across the table, grab him by the collar and begin pummeling his pudgy face. It took a moment to find the words to answer his question. "I can understand your concern, of course, but I believe she was focused on her son and the sudden appearance of police officers crashing a simple fishing trip on a relaxed Saturday afternoon. Nothing more." I continued to display a quiet smile.

"Okay, if you say so," Hearn replied. I thought I caught a hint of sarcasm in his voice, but maintained my outwardly calm demeanor. "And really, at this point we have no idea what more we're gonna find once we start digging—or I guess I should say diving—into the investigation." Sgt. Eason chuckled at the obvious joke. I did not react.

Still quietly furious, I left and drove slowly back to the mental safety of my apartment behind the gallery in Savannah. I needed to calm down, to relax, to quit trying to think—or overthink—the implications of the shoe. First and foremost, there was no confirmation that the objects I had seen inside it were in fact human bones. And if they were confirmed to be so, a logical explanation might be that someone had decided to go fishing without asking the permission of the Dawsons and accidentally drowned. The property was in the middle of nowhere. There are alligators in this part of the state. Perhaps he was dragged into the water and disappeared without a trace. I imagined by the end of the next day the mystery would be well on the way to being solved. Tragic perhaps, but end of story. A few more days and life would be back to normal. It was getting late as I arrived back at the gallery. I parked the pickup in the carriage house garage and headed upstairs to try to calm down and relax.

I slept well and spent most of the next day worrying about my relationship with Jenna. It was probably a silly thought, but I imagined that she would call, apologize for the way she had reacted to Saturday's events, and ask me to come see her. Nothing happened. By four o'clock I had given up on my fantasies and, following Mrs. Dawson's suggestion, decided to call Jenna.

The call immediately went to voicemail. I pressed "End" without leaving a message.

I waited five minutes, then ten, trying to decide if I should call back. I made the decision not to, and was walking out the door when my phone vibrated. Jenna's number appeared on the screen. I said, "Hello." She replied with a soft, "Hey." There was a moment of silence, then, "Oh, John, I am so sorry. I..., I don't know what I was thinking yesterday, and I acted like a complete fool. I wanted to call you last night, but I was too embarrassed—ashamed, really—and was afraid I'd start crying. And then I saw you were calling a few minutes ago, and...."

"You don't have to explain. I know you were upset...."

"It wasn't really you," Jenna said, "it was the whole situation. My little boy, sitting there all alone, with you and the cops standing off to the side talking. And...," her voice trailed off.

"I understand. It's okay. I love you."

"And I love you...," Jenna said.

"Why don't we get together later this coming week, when

things have maybe calmed down a little? I'll pick you up and we can go out to dinner, if Robert can stay at your parents."

"Sounds good," Jenna said meekly.

"Fine, I'll call you late tomorrow afternoon," I said, not mentioning that I planned to spend much of the day at the Dawson pond with the sheriff and the divers.

On Monday morning I headed for Evans County in the pickup, being sure to leave before Jessica, my one full-time employee at the gallery, showed up for work and demanded an explanation of why I was driving it. I timed my departure to be at the farm by about 9:00 a.m., about when Sheriff Hearn had told me the divers would arrive. I pulled up at the gate to find it propped open and the grassy area next to the pond hosting a jumble of vehicles, including three sheriff's patrol cars, several cars with Florida tags, and a large white Mercedes Sprinter van whose windowless sides were emblazoned with "Underwater Archeology," a schematic illustration of a scuba diver, and a Perry, Florida, address and phone number. Hearn was engaged in a conversation with a muscular white-haired man garbed in a black wetsuit, complete with hood. A second man in a wetsuit observed while two other men appeared to be assembling some sort of underwater rig with lights and a video camera encased in a waterproof housing. The sheriff spied me driving up and waved me over.

"Mr. O'Toole, I want you to meet Barry Frank, the genius behind this crew of fellows." The white-haired man stuck out his hand and mumbled something about being pleased to meet me. "Barry's been in the forensic diving business for a long time. He and his guys are the best. I've sort of told them what you discovered, and what I think we all understand we're looking for. Possibly a body," he paused, "or body parts." Frank remained expressionless. "I want you to show him exactly where the boy snagged the shoe, and they'll take it from there. Now, they understand the possibility that something they find may end up as evidence, they're going to try to do it 'right,' as they say. I'll let Barry give you the details."

Frank began by thanking me for my help and explained that there would be no more than two divers in the lake at any given time. "It's pretty dark and murky in this kind of water, so the lead diver carries a battery-powered searchlight, and the other diver follows along with the camera rig. We'll be shooting high resolution video of anything important that we find, and if we need still photos, we can get them from the video." He said he wanted me to tell him exactly where I thought they should start the search.

Ten minutes later Frank, now wearing a face mask and a compressed air cylinder strapped to his back, waded gingerly into the water where I had reeled in the shoe. The water at the mid-portion of the dam was fourteen or fifteen feet deep, according to what Mr. Dawson told the sheriff. By six feet out from the shoreline both divers were waist-deep in water, at which point they began their search. The rest of us stood on the bank, tracing the lines of bubbles as the divers systematically moved back and forth over the bottom. The entire dam was perhaps 200 to 250 feet in length and wide enough to serve as a narrow road to the other side if anyone were foolish enough to attempt driving across it. We moved as a group along the dam, following the trails of bubbles as they moved into progressively deeper water. Approximately forty feet from the lake shore, the motion of the bubble trails stopped, often merging and seeming to remain in one area. After about five minutes, Frank's head popped up as he treaded water to maintain his position. Removing the regulator from his mouth, he yelled, "I think we've got something. We're going to take some video then head back to the shore. Sheriff, I want you to get a good look at things before we decide what to do next."

Hearn turned to me and nodded as if to say, "I told you so."

For the next fifteen minutes the bubble trails stayed in a relatively small area, then rapidly headed back toward the bank where both divers had entered the water. Frank emerged first, then the cameraman, both shedding their fins, tanks and masks. One of his other men had opened the back door of the van, lowered a folding shelf, and set up a laptop connected to a high-resolution video monitor. He removed the camera from its waterproof case and extracted a memory card which he inserted in a slot on the side of the laptop. Frank sat down on a small stool in front of the computer and began to scroll through the video. After about two minutes, he yelled, "How about coming in here, Sheriff, and let me show you what we've found." Hearn motioned for me to follow him.

In the semi-darkness of the van's interior, Frank narrated as shadowy shapes floated across the screen. "Okay, here we are roughly thirty-five or forty feet out from the bank, in water that's around twelve feet deep. You can only see about eighteen inches or so in the water, so we had to move slowly without disturbing the mud on the bottom." Pointing at the video, he continued, "Now watch this as we move forward." We were silent as the image advanced across the bottom of the pond. A Coca-Cola can briefly appeared on screen then faded from view. Abruptly, a linear whitish object appeared, apparently catching the cameraman's attention. "That, fellows, appears to be a human bone, probably a femur. And...," he was interrupted by the murmur of multiple voices as the word was passed to the gaggle of deputies and dive crew standing just outside the van's open back doors.

"And," Frank continued as the video moved slowly ahead, "that bluish object there may be a piece of clothing—presumably synthetic fabric, of course—and just here," he pointed at another whitish object on the screen, "is what appears to be a skull, or part of a skull. Some of it is buried in mud." Again, the murmur of voices rose and fell.

Sheriff Hearn asked, "Barry, go back a bit to where you saw that piece of cloth or clothing or something. I want to ask about one thing there."

Frank slowly reversed the video until Hearn, pointing at the screen, said, "What is that, right there? Looks like it's got oblong circles or something on it."

Frank studied the object for a moment, then said, "I'm not sure. We'd need a closer look, but right offhand I'd guess it's a heavy chain, you know, like a logging chain. Whoever dumped the body here had to have something to weigh it down."

CHAPTER 6

There was little doubt now that the depths of the Dawson pond held the remains of a murder victim. There was much to be done before that became an official assessment, accompanied for sure by massive turmoil injected into the family's otherwise peaceful life. The oaks and the pines, the grassy bit of pasture, the secluded beauty of the sunlight reflecting off the water, had now become witnesses at a crime scene, their idyllic beauty soon to be ripped away by waves of law enforcement investigators. But there was more yet to come....

Barry Frank, still sitting in front of the computer, turned to the sheriff saying, "Before we get too distracted by the chain or whatever that is, there's something else you need to see." He tapped on the keyboard, advanced the video back to where it had displayed what he thought was a skull, and then resumed the play. "Okay, now we're moving ahead here maybe three feet or so and we come across this." He pointed at another ill-defined white shape seemingly embedded in the mud. His gloved hand entered the frame as he reached out and gently swished the muck and debris off the object. As the murky water slowly cleared, the empty eye sockets of a second skull stared back at the camera. "There's at least one more body," Frank said. "We decided at that point that we'd discovered enough. This is something for the crime lab guys." This time, rather than the murmur of voices, those of us staring at the screen looked on in shocked silence.

As the scuba crew gathered up their gear, the sheriff and Frank huddled at a distance next to the overturned boat moored to the oak tree. After a brief exchange of words, they called me over to join them. Hearn spoke. "John, I don't really understand why Nate Dawson didn't want to be here this morning. I told him we'd have a crowd of folks here and what we'd be doing, and was real clear about the problems that were gonna crop up if we found a body. He didn't seem concerned, said that Mondays were his busiest day at work, and that you would probably want to be here since you were the one who'd 'opened this can of worms.' Those were his exact words. I think now he needs to drop everything and get his sorry butt out here. Looks like we've got two bodies, and it's pretty clear that we'll need to call in the GBI and the crime lab folks to work the scene. And as Barry here says, they're gonna need to drain the pond to see what else is down there. Not sure right now how that's gonna get done, but we'll figure it out."

Things just kept getting worse. "I'll be glad to talk with Mr. Dawson, but you're the one who needs to call him first and explain the situation," I said. "I don't think they're especially happy with me because of what happened with Jenna's kid. I'll back you up, but I need to keep a low profile. Seems like he's forgetting that finding the shoe just happened. I didn't plan it. If I hadn't taken Robert fishing, we wouldn't have found it, and none of us would be here now."

Hearn seemed to consider my words for a brief moment, then said, "Sounds okay. I'll take care of it." He paused, then, "Are you gonna stick around?"

"No, I've caused enough trouble. I'd appreciate it though if you'd call me later and keep me up to date on what you find."

"You know that violates protocol," he replied, looking serious.

"I know, but it's probably the least you can do."

"Okay," Hearn said, "but all this is confidential and off the record."

I thanked him, shook his hand, and headed back to the

Dawsons to exchange their pickup for my car. I took the long route driving there, presuming by the time I arrived the sheriff would have contacted Mr. Dawson, who would have in turn called his wife, who probably would have said something to their daughter. I could imagine Jenna now, screaming at me that the fish Robert could have brought home to eat were grown in water fertilized by rotting human flesh. It was probably the end of our relationship. The old adage about "the road to hell being paved with good intentions" popped into my mind. I had blown it. I needed to hang my head, tuck my tail between my legs, and start thinking once again about putting the pieces of my life back together.

Arriving at the Dawsons, I saw my car parked in the driveway, and the rear of Mrs. Dawson's visible under the carport. Mr. Dawson's work truck was nowhere to be seen. That was either good or bad, I couldn't decide. I parked the old Chevy pickup on the curb and rang the doorbell at the carport entrance. Mrs. Dawson appeared shortly, a sad smile on her face. "Oh, John, this is all so terrible. I am so very, very sorry to have you involved in all this." She seemed to genuinely mean her words. "Nate just called me from work and filled me in about finding two bodies in the pond. Can you believe that? All these years we've been having family gatherings there with the kids fishing and swimming and all. What if they had found a bone or a skull or something…?" Her voice trailed off as she pictured the scene in her thoughts. "I know that finding the shoe was just a stroke of luck, or fate, or whatever you call it, but I think we really owe you a debt of gratitude, especially in the way you handled it." For a very brief moment I thought her words might be bitterly sarcastic, but she smiled and waited for my reply.

"I just am worried about the way things happened with

Jenna...."

"Oh, John, she's a mother, and a protective one at that. She's been so worried about Robert growing up without a father figure there for him, and was just over the moon when you volunteered to take him fishing. I haven't seen her that happy in a while. And then when you called and said there were some problems, she imagined the worst, that Robert had been injured or bitten by a snake, and rushed out there without calling you first. She said when she saw the police were there she believed something terrible had happened—her first thought was to take Robert back to the security of home. She told me later how embarrassed she was. And when you called before Nate and I were still trying to figure out what had happened. It's clear now that you did the right thing, and again, I thank you." Mrs. Dawson stepped over and, for the first time since I started seeing Jenna, hugged me. "Jenna was still in a tizzy, so that's why I sounded the way I did. I've talked with her several times since then and I think everything is okay now."

I was feeling considerably more assured. "Did the sheriff tell you that he's going to call in the Georgia Bureau of Investigation? Or that they would likely have to drain the pond somehow?"

"He told Nate, and Nate told me. I hate it, of course. That property has been in my family for more than a hundred years. My great granddaddy was in the timber and turpentine business back then, owned a lot of land and was rather wealthy, or so I'm told. When things went bad in the Depression, he managed to keep that little farm—it's only about 225 acres—but lost everything else."

"So the land was in your family...?" I asked. Not that it mattered, but I had assumed it was inherited from Mr. Dawson's side.

"Yes, but that was years and years ago. We're just like everybody else these days, paycheck-to-paycheck. Frankly, the pond was the only real luxury we had." She paused again, glancing out the window for a moment with a wistful look on her face. "Hope this storm blows over real soon."

"Did the sheriff say where the investigation is going next?"

Mrs. Dawson flashed a quick frown replying, "Not really. He filled us in a bit Saturday and then called not long ago to let us know the latest. He said they're going to want to interview anybody and everybody that might have had access to that property over the last several years. What they do and where things go depends on what the investigators find next, he says. The pond's been there for years and years. Those skeletons could be a hundred years old or more. Lord only knows what happened way back when…."

"That may be," I said, thinking that the popularity of Nike athletic shoes and the polyester clothing seen by the scuba crew made it far more likely that the bodies were dumped there in the last few years.

"If they haven't been there that long," Mrs. Dawson continued, "I'm not sure I can recall all the people, all the names. We had parties there. Nate used to let his friends fish there every now and then. Jenna used to take her friends from high school and college there sometimes…. It's just too much to try to remember."

It bothered me to hear Jenna's name mentioned once again.

CHAPTER 7

I was back at the gallery in Savannah by late afternoon, just in time to check in with Jessica before she left for the day. As usual on Mondays, business had been slow. A couple of interior designers dropped by, as well as the usual tourists. We sold enough to meet expenses, but not much more. I thought it best at this point to take a wait-and-see attitude about the Dawsons' pond. I hoped to hear from Sheriff Hearn, but was not at all sure he would follow up on his promise to keep me informed. To my surprise, I received a call from Nate Dawson just as I was rummaging through my refrigerator looking for something to eat for supper. He said he wanted to talk with me privately about "helping out with this problem" at the pond, and asked if he could meet me in Savannah late the next afternoon. We arranged to meet at the gallery at about six o'clock.

Just before the appointed time, Nate pulled his pickup into the courtyard behind the gallery, still wearing his work clothes and appearing somewhat nervous. Once securely settled in my private office, I began the conversation by asking, "What can I do to help you?"

"I had a long talk with Sheriff Hearn," he said, "and I realize there's no other way to do things. There's at least two bodies down on the bottom of the pond, and he says he thinks they're probably murder victims—but he can't be sure. He's calling in the GBI and the crime lab, and said he's been working on getting the water out of the pond. They're planning on bringing in some big diesel-powered pumps instead of breaking the dam. Whole thing may take weeks. Or longer."

"I know that. So, tell me how I can help."

"Well, I asked the sheriff if they had any suspects, and he

said they didn't, but just about anybody who's been around that pond in god knows when is gonna be looked at real hard. He said that and looked at me to kinda see how I would react, and then he said that I was welcome to bring a lawyer with me if I was concerned the investigators might do things they weren't supposed to do, or if I had other worries about the bodies. I don't know what he meant by 'other worries,' but I'm athinking he may be suspicious of me."

I wasn't sure how to react to Nate's comment. Was his concern prompted by something he did not want discovered? I just could not see him as a murderer. Were there other things? I tried a neutral response. "Tell me more about that."

"Well, over the years sometimes my buddies—my married buddies—want to meet their girlfriends somewhere..., somewhere real private, you know...." I nodded, thinking I knew where this was going. "And, I feel like I gotta be real honest with the sheriff, and I don't want...."

I cut him off, saying, "I understand. Maybe you could just...."

"I want you to be there with me. You're a lawyer, and you know how these things work. I don't want to get trapped into saying something I shouldn't, but I don't want to hold back anything that would help find out if them's murder victims or...."

"Nate, I was a lawyer, but I don't have a license now and...."

"But you know when to tell me to stop talking, or whatever, or to tell the sheriff or whoever when to stop asking them kinds of questions. I've seen how they do it on TV shows."

"But Mrs. Dawson said that land was inherited from her side of the family. Shouldn't they talk with her, too?"

Dawson rolled his eyes. "Lord, she's scared to death of

sitting there and getting grilled by the police. She told the sheriff I was gonna be the family spokesman, and I said I'd do that, and then when I got to thinking about it I figured out I better talk with you to help me out, to back me up."

"What does Jenna think about all this?"

"I haven't asked her, but it's none of her concern."

"She told me some of her high school and college friends have been out there years ago. They might have the lock code and...."

"Ain't nothing to that. I told the sheriff she wasn't gonna talk with him unless he got a court order. He kinda backed off then."

We talked for a few minutes longer, but Dawson seemed to have gotten what he wanted, my agreement to make sure he did not say something to the investigators that he shouldn't. I was certain that he had no involvement in secreting the bodies in the lake, so I would basically be holding his hand. If his buddies and their extramarital affairs were exposed, that was their problem, not Nate's. He left after no more than half an hour's visit.

About two hours later I was reading a book when Dawson called to say the sheriff had notified him the crime lab folks had looked over the scene and that an industrial contractor they had hired would be setting up the pumps the following afternoon. I told him I would drive over late Wednesday to see how things were going. There was nothing I could do or say; this was just moral support. But if things ever did manage to work out between Jenna and me, he would be my father-in-law. Best not to miss the opportunity.

It was nearly four o'clock Wednesday afternoon before I made it back to Evans County and the Dawson pond. The scene had changed dramatically. The dirt track leading to the small pasture was now a muddy ribbon, and the small pasture area occupied by several trucks. My car, the nearly two-decade old Lincoln I had inherited from my grandmother, slithered its way through the mud, barely managing to avoid getting stuck. I was greeted with the smell of diesel exhaust and what sounded like a fleet of eighteen-wheelers idling, the source of which turned out to be two large pumps at the far end of the dam. Two large-diameter orange hoses snaked their way into the pond, whose water level had dropped by two to three feet since the pumps were started about twenty-four hours earlier. Nate Dawson and the sheriff stood on the dam, observing. They waved me over. "Hey, John," Dawson said. "We've been expecting you." He seemed quite at ease now.

"Looks like you've got things underway," I said.

"Yep," the sheriff spoke. "Pond's down a good bit, and we're going to continue to run the pumps until it's mostly dry. I've posted two deputies here to keep a close eye on things 'round the clock, and two of the pump contractor's guys are here to keep the pumps fueled and running. They figure two or three more days max, and then we'll see where we need to go. The Savannah state crime lab is on standby and will have a team out here within a couple of hours once we give them a call. I've talked to my contact at the GBI, and they'll also be able to get someone here on short notice. Come on over here and let me show you what we've got going on."

I followed them to the other end of the dam where the pumps had been placed on a concrete spillway. The pond water was being discharged into a stream bed below the dam. The newly revealed lake bottom just below the former waterline was unremarkable except for an occasional sunken limb and a few cans and bottles tossed in the water over the decades. "The bodies were seen over there," Hearn pointed, "so we're easing the water down from the opposite side, only taking it a little at a time to avoid disturbing any possible clues." He paused and surveyed the expanse of water. "Nothing yet, but we'll see. I hope two bodies will be all...." Nate Dawson frowned.

I spent a few more minutes in conversation with the two, then headed into town to see Jenna. I had not spent a private moment with her since the discovery of the shoe and wanted some quiet, personal downtime with nothing major lurking in the background. When I'd called earlier she said Robert would be spending the night with her parents, and I was welcome to stay at her place if I wanted to.

It was almost six by the time I reached Jenna's apartment. The door was unlocked so I let myself in, noting immediately the aroma of candlewood, and the sound of a blender coming from the direction of the kitchen. "Hey!" I yelled.

Jenna stuck her head out. She was wearing an apron. "Hey, to you. Sit down and relax. I'm trying to fix you a special dinner to make up for the bitch I've been all week."

"You haven't been a bitch. We've both just had a lot going on. We're good."

"I know, but I feel like we need to find something to take our minds off whatever that 'lot' is, so I'm working on chicken parmesan, with a good salad and a bottle of Italian white wine whose name I can't pronounce, but the man at the store said it was the best." Jenna grinned.

It was starting to look like a perfect evening.

CHAPTER 8

And it was nearly a perfect evening, mostly because we talked, laughed and loved, never once mentioning the Dawson pond, or murder, or Robert. After a good night's sleep and a light breakfast, I was back on Highway 280, headed toward Savannah in time to arrive by nine o'clock. The day went smoothly. Jessica was in a good mood and, contrary to her usual curiosity, did not ask about Jenna or why I had been spending so much time in Claxton. I was anticipating a similarly peaceful day on Friday, a delusion that was shattered by an urgent mid-afternoon phone call from Nate Dawson. "John, are you free? I know I'm asking a lot, but can you get over here as quick as you can? I'm at the pond."

"Uh, yeah, I believe so…," I said, even though I was in the middle of a conversation with Hattie, the gallery's long-time bookkeeper. "What's going on?"

"I don't want to talk about it on the phone, but something's come up. Several things." His voice was tense and pressured. "I just need your advice. And help." Apparently speaking to someone nearby I heard him say, "Hang on just a minute. I'm on the phone." Then to me, "They found some more things in the pond and I'm not sure how to handle it. The sheriff's called the crime lab and the GBI and they're supposed to be on the way here now—probably get here before you do. I know they're gonna want to interview me and I don't want to do no talking without you here to keep me out of trouble."

I said I'd leave immediately and try to be there in a bit more than an hour. Dawson hung up without saying goodbye. I took I-16 this time, thinking that I could probably get away with eighty miles per hour and shave off a few minutes. The sheriff had mentioned that the pond should be mostly dry by Friday, so whatever had been revealed must have caused Dawson's frantic call. I arrived just in time to see an Evans County dump truck exiting the gate on the dirt road. Apparently, the county had brought in several loads of gravel to make the track to the pond passible to heavier traffic. To my surprise, most of the vehicles that were in the small pasture earlier were now gone; only Nate Dawson's work truck and half a dozen sedans with government license plates remained. A loose huddle of a dozen or so men were gathered in the middle of the dam, looking down on the now mostly empty lake bottom. Despite the distance I recognized Hearn and Dawson waving and beckoning me to join them.

I parked on the newly laid gravel and walked toward the group. As I drew closer, I thought I recognized Pete Marsh, a Savannah homicide detective I had met and worked with in the city several months earlier. Instead of his usual suit and tie, this time he was dressed in khaki pants, boots and a shirt emblazoned with an embroidered image of the state seal and the words "Georgia Bureau of Investigation." Sheriff Hearn and Nate Dawson stepped out of the group and welcomed me with firm handshakes. "A lot can change in a couple of days, John," Hearn said. "Nate wanted you here before we got started. And—to my surprise—there's someone here who says he knows you well. Had a lot of good things to say about you." Dawson smiled and nodded but said nothing. He looked nervous.

As he spoke, Pete Marsh stepped over with a firm handshake. "Good to see you again, John. I have to say though, I didn't think it would be under these circumstances. Trouble does seem to follow you around."

"Pete, what are you doing here? I thought you were on the road to running the show with the Savannah police."

"Long story that we can save for later. I just thought I'd enjoy working with the GBI. Better pay, better benefits, less politics. So, they hired me...."

"And we're damned glad we did," a gray-haired man stepped up. "I'm Nelson Jackson, with the GBI's Investigative Division. Pete is being assigned to this case. I'm just here to...."

"Nelson's my boss," Pete interrupted. "Showing me the ropes, as they say."

"He's one of the best," Jackson said. "We were fortunate to snag him from the SPD. He speaks highly of you."

With the introductions done, the sheriff said, "Let's all walk over to the spot of pasture there and let me say a few words. I'm then going to turn this over to our friends from the crime lab and the GBI. I want everyone to understand at the outset where we're planning on going with what may be evidence related to a mass murder." It was the first time I had heard the term mentioned.

Even though the day was cool, we stood in the late-afternoon shade of an ancient oak tree while Sheriff Hearn spoke. "We all have gotten a bit acquainted with one another, and we all know why we're here. Six days ago, this gentleman to my right here," he gestured toward me, "was taking a young boy fishing and snagged onto a Nike athletic shoe that contained what appeared to be human bones. I requested the assistance of a group of forensic divers and—without disturbing anything, mind you—we looked at the area of the lake where the shoe was hooked and discovered two skeletonized bodies on the bottom. At that point, I notified you fellows from the GBI and the crime lab to be on alert as we pumped the water out of the pond. That was completed for the most part earlier today, and we'll turn the pumps on again if more water accumulates.

"What we've all seen just now," he continued, gesturing toward the dam, "is the discovery of what appear to be at least two more skeletonized bodies visible near the site where the first two were discovered. Now, we've not gone down there poking around—we're going to leave that to the crime lab folks here so we don't destroy any evidence. And since Evans County has a population of less than eleven thousand citizens and limited resources, it's clear that we need the state's support, which is why I've called you in to assist us—to take over the investigation, really. That's a step down the road, of course. While we assume a crime—or crimes—were committed, we need to understand as best we can, who the deceased were, when and how they died, and of course, who killed them, if they were in fact murdered.

"So, here are our plans. First, we're keeping the pumps here and one man to attend to them twenty-four hours a day, if needed. Second, the crime lab crew," he gestured in their direction, "will be bringing in first thing tomorrow morning a couple of vans with mobile work stations to document, sort and classify what they find on, near or around the bodies here—I'm not calling them victims just yet, not until we're sure. And third, while we—the Evans County Sheriff's Department—will remain on the case, the GBI will be taking over the primary investigative duties. That team will be led by Pete Marsh, an experienced homicide detective who was formerly a member of the Savannah police force.

"Although you know this, I want to remind you once again that this is private property owned by the Dawson family of Claxton. Mr. Nate Dawson is here and will be glad to answer any informal questions to the best of his knowledge. And he will be assisted and advised by John O'Toole, a family friend of the Dawsons." He pointed at me. "Mr. O'Toole is a previous acquaintance of Agent Marsh, who vouches for him and his integrity. I know that I do not have to remind you that as this is an ongoing investigation, you should not speak with other persons about what has been discovered here or anything at all related to this search. In particular that includes reporters or members of the media. The roadside gate will remain closed at all times while the crime lab folks are here. I've already handed out my business cards. They have my cell number on them, so feel free to call me any time day or night if you have questions. And of course I'll be in and out of here several times a day checking on things." With that, the small crowd spread out, most heading back to their vehicles to return home.

Sheriff Hearn, with Nate Dawson meekly following a couple of feet behind him, walked over to where I was talking to Pete Marsh and asked, "You want to see what showed up when the water dropped?" Pete said he needed to get home, but that he presumed he'd be seeing more of me as the investigation progressed. We walked to where the group had been standing on the dam when I first arrived. As the sun sank lower in the sky, beams of light filtered through the trees surrounding the pond, casting a dappled pattern on the muddy lake bottom. About twenty-five or thirty feet out from the old shoreline on the dam I could make out a patch of blue, perhaps the bit of clothing I had seen earlier on the divers' video.

Hearn pointed, "See that blue object there?" I nodded. "Okay, just a few feet to the right of it is an off-white object. That's the first skull we saw. And about six feet or more to the left is another skull, the one whose eye sockets you could see on the video. Now if you'll look about ten feet more to the left," he pointed, "there are a few whitish objects looking like they're lined up. That's a section of human spine. And just beyond that you can see another piece of spine and a smooth thing that looks like a large rock. That's the back side of the skull of a fourth body." Hearn paused as I squinted, taking in the terrible magnitude of what appeared to be the remains of four human bodies, discarded and forgotten.

I turned to him and said, "Why? And who?"

"That's what we all want to know," he replied.

I glanced at Nate Dawson. He was staring fixedly at the remains on the bottom of the pond. Silent tears were streaming from his eyes.

CHAPTER 9

I was uneasy. Or upset, or worried, or distraught—I didn't know how to describe the way I felt. Earlier in the day, I had rushed to the pond in response to Nate Dawson's call. Now I took the long way home, driving slowly in the creeping twilight, heeding the speed limit of fifty-five as I tossed the events of the past week back and forth in my mind. How could a simple fishing trip with Jenna's son have turned into a mass-murder investigation? Or was there another, less dreadful explanation for the remains of the four unknown individuals? Who were they? What did they have in common? A lyric from a Bob Segar song playing softly on the satellite radio poked its way into my consciousness: "...workin' on mysteries without any clues...." The perfect description for my situation. Less than a week ago I was on top of the world. Now, six days later, I felt like I was knocking on the gates of hell. Something was going to happen, but I had no idea what that might be.

Two vans from the Savannah state crime laboratory were arriving just as I was leaving the site. I had asked Pete Marsh earlier how long he thought it would be before the techs finished their work. He said he did not know, but it was certainly going to be a couple of weeks there at the scene, and then weeks or even months back at the lab. "I would hesitate to guess, John, but the whole process is rather standard. First, recover everything from the scene that might have a bearing on the case. Second, analyze what you've discovered: the dirt the bodies are found in, the clothing they were wearing if any survived, evidence of trauma, including broken bones or gunshot wounds, and so on. And then the lab work comes in, if there's an indication. In this case, we'd hope to be able to do DNA testing, but a lot of that depends on whether or not a good sample is available, or if the time underwater has destroyed what was there." He paused, thinking. "I'd say the info will come out in dribs and drabs. In a week or thereabouts, we'll know the sex and the approximate age of the remains. In two or three, the lab will either have a clear cause of death or call it 'indeterminate.' Depends on what they find. With the DNA, it could take days, or weeks, or months, it's complicated. What the lab will be looking for, though, is what they call the 'magic key,' the one single thing that breaks open the whole case. I remember one situation we had in Savannah when some fishermen found a corpse floating in the river. It was a gang-related killing. The victim's head and the hands had been cut off to try to prevent an ID, and his DNA didn't match anyone in the system. But he had a single key in his front pants pocket—guess the crew that killed him missed it when they searched him before dumping his body. We traced it to a certain hardware store that had security cameras. Got a photo of the victim, and as it turned out, the two other guys who were later convicted of his murder. That's the 'magic key,' the sort of thing the crime lab hopes to find."

To Pete Marsh, for whom I held great respect, and the many others who were and would be working on this case, the challenge was a problem that had to be solved. But from my perspective, it was potentially another massive obstacle between me and my relationship with Jenna.

A week passed, then ten days. I kept in touch with Jenna, who drove to Savannah and spent one night with me during the week. Other than a casual mention, we didn't speak about what had now become the silent-elephant in the room, the investigation going on at the family pond. On the surface all seemed well between us, but I still worried. Mrs. Dawson called several times to ask if I had heard anything from the sheriff or the GBI or anyone else. She said her husband had tried to visit the pond but had twice been turned away by Evans County deputies with the excuse that the crime lab techs were "working the scene." Not surprisingly, she seemed concerned.

On Tuesday, a week and a half later, Pete Marsh called. "I wanted to fill you in on what the crime lab has come up with before I call the Dawsons. It's complicated and confusing, and since they've indicated you're working with them, I thought it would be all right if you could answer any follow-up questions they have. I've been really busy, and it'd be a great help to me." I said I'd be glad to fill in the gaps. "There's nothing here thus far that's truly confidential," Pete continued, "in fact—I'm not sure when—we're going to make some public announcements asking folks to call our tip lines if they have any information that might have bearing on the case." I could hear the rustling of papers as he took a deep breath. "I tell you, John, this has got to be one of the most bizarre cases I've ever worked in my twenty-five-plus years in law enforcement." A chill seemed to run over my body.

"Okay," Pete began. "As you saw when we were there the other day, there appeared to be remains of four bodies. The lab has labeled them as A through D, with A being the body to whom the shoe y'all snagged belongs, B being the second set of remains discovered by the divers, C is the one where the spine was about the only thing you could see from the bank, and D is the one with both the spine and skull visible. Got that?" I said I did.

"They are all male and appear to have been there for a number of years. The lab is certain they were not dumped at the same time. They don't have a close estimate on that as yet, but they're guessing the last one was placed there about six years ago but they say it could have three or four years earlier. Age-wise, the youngest is Victim A, the one with the shoe—they found the other one, by the way—he's thought to be between about eighteen and twenty-five and appears to have likely died of a gunshot wound. He had a 9 mm bullet lodged in his spine at an angle that suggests it would have passed through his heart. He's the only one of the four for whom they've found a tentative cause of death.

"Victims B and C appear to be around forty-five, give or take a few years, and Victim D is older, maybe in his fifties or early sixties. The lab's still working on potential causes of death for those three, but they do feel confident based on sediments covering the remains that Victim A was dumped first, then Victims B and C, and after that Victim D." Pete paused then added, "They keep stressing though the timing of the presumed murders is really a guess.

"There are plenty of other potential clues that the lab is still processing. All four appear to have been fully clothed when placed in the water, but cloth with an organic makeup such as cotton or wool decays away rapidly. The shoe you found and the blue polo shirt Victim A was wearing were all synthetic, so they've held up well. The lab folks tell me that athletic shoes can be easy to date because companies like Nike or Adidas or Reebok change styles so often that sometimes it's possible to know approximately when they were purchased. That may help ID that poor fellow.

"And there are other things. Victims B and D appear to be wearing wedding bands. One was plain, but the other was engraved on the inside with initials and a date. That's being followed up. Now here's a possible clue: the ones they're calling B and C were both weighted down with concrete blocks and three-eights-inch steel cables that seem to come from the same source, suggesting they were dumped at the same time. The other two were weighted down with heavy logging chains. Give the lab another couple of weeks and maybe we'll know more."

"What was it you said about asking for the public's help?" I asked.

"Just that, but it's going to be several weeks or longer before we do. First thing, we've got to get a better handle on what all we know from the crime scene, and then figure out how much we can make public without damaging the case. We're planning on briefly describing what we know and asking anyone with information to call a special number we're setting up." He hesitated, then, "Yeah, it's a two-edged sword for sure. Every nut case in the state will be calling up to tell us they know who the victims are, or who killed them and why. In my experience about ninety-nine percent of what you get is total speculation or fantasy, or some guy trying to get his obnoxious neighbor arrested, but there's that one percent...."

"...The magic key." I finished the sentence for him.

"Yeah."

"Are you going to try to get TV coverage, social media, that kind of thing?"

"Reluctantly, yeah." I thought I heard Pete sigh. "We don't want to sensationalize this, but you've got to back off and think about it. These men, the ones we're calling the victims, they were living, breathing human beings with families and jobs and relationships, and all that goes along with being alive in this crazy world. And even though we don't yet know their identities, who they were, they had to have just disappeared from the face of the earth one day, leaving wives and children and employers and friends to wonder what happened. Once we make an ID, I suspect there are going to be a whole bunch of folks out there who, after they get over the shock and sadness of knowing what became of a friend or husband, will say 'Thank you. It's sad, but now at least I know what happened.'"

CHAPTER 10

As often happens, the GBI's plan to keep both the investigation and its secrets confidential was destined to fail. Whoever leaked the details would remain a matter of speculation, but the fact that the public soon knew was abundantly evident. Following Pete's call, I planned to wait until he'd had a chance to contact the Dawsons, then call them myself to see if I could answer any questions or otherwise be of help. I made my first call to their home phone about an hour later, but got a busy signal. A second, third and fourth try over the next half hour yielded the same result. As I was about to call a fifth time, my cell rang as the Dawsons' number popped up on the screen. I heard Mrs. Dawson's voice, high-pitched and strained, "John, what is happening? Why are all these people calling us wanting to know what's going on at the pond? They keep asking about dead bodies, and murder and…."

"Has Pete Marsh talked with you this morning?" I interrupted.

"Who is he?" she asked, "The GBI man? No, but when he does I want to give him a piece of my mind."

"I spoke with him earlier. He said he was about to call you and fill you in on what the crime lab folks have found."

"Well, he hasn't. Or maybe I should say he's probably tried but the phone's been busy for the last two hours. We've had about ten phone calls from friends and people we know, and five or six calls from other people who say they are with a television station, or radio, or newspaper or whatever. I've just been hanging up on those kinds because I don't know who they really are. They all keep asking about the bodies. What bodies? Why does everyone know something that we don't and why hasn't anyone called us?"

"Mrs. Dawson, Agent Marsh called me earlier this morning and gave me an update on what they had found at your family's pond. He was going to call you right away, but I guess your line has been busy. He's all wrapped up with the investigation, and he wanted to fill me in so I could answer any questions you might have. I guess he couldn't get through to you with so many people calling your house. You really do need to talk with him, but I can tell you briefly what's been going on...." With that I spent the next few minutes describing the crime lab's findings thus far. I finished with, "I know that's a lot to take in, but is there anything you want me to go over, anything that's not clear?"

My question was greeted by silence. I could hear her breathing heavily on the other end of the line, then, "Are you telling me that my family's pond, the place we have made so many wonderful memories over the years, has become a dumping ground, a..., a...," she searched for a word, "a garbage disposal for dead people?"

"It's not...," I began.

"That was the one fine thing we had. The one thing in our simple life we could enjoy and be proud of and share with our friends. We've had church picnics there. The kids when they were little used to swim in the pond. Did Jenna ever tell you how much that place meant to her? Gosh, we even had her wedding there with that sorry Carl she made the mistake of marrying. We tried so hard to make it a special place, and now...." She did not finish her sentence.

"I'm sorry," I said.

"Not your fault," she replied before the line went dead.

I called Pete Marsh's cell. He answered with, "I know why you're calling, John, and I'm just as pissed as I suspect you are.

I...."

"Where are you?" I interrupted.

"I'm at the pond. I want you to listen to something." A few seconds later I could hear what sounded like the distant buzzing of insects. Putting the phone back to his ear Marsh asked, "Recognize that?"

"I don't know—a swarm of bees, maybe?"

"No, drones. Two of them now, but there was a third earlier. They're from the news vans parked up on the dirt road. A couple of deputies are up there now telling whoever is flying them to take 'em down immediately or get arrested. I'm sure they'll hear some 'freedom of the press' BS in response." Marsh paused. "Must have worked. They're both flying back toward the road."

"What happened, Pete?" I asked. "How did the news get out?"

"It's like swamp gas, John. Bubbles start in the muck and manage to find their way to the top. Probably some deputy went home and after a few beers tells his wife—after warning her not to say anything to anyone—about what's going on. And she gets all excited and tells her hairdresser who's dating some guy from the radio station and tells him, but he wants a job at the TV station so to improve his chances gives them the tip and offers to show them where to go fly their drones and so on.... Really, such crap is almost expected, and the spies and gossips rarely get any confidential information, but...." He spoke to someone nearby saying, "Yes, we will arrest him. Make damned sure he knows that," then resumed talking to me, "...but letting the world know what's going on also lets the guilty party, or parties, know as well. Sometimes they skip, or make sure they've covered their tracks, or start trying to intimidate potential witnesses. Just makes our jobs all that much more difficult. I need to run, gotta take care of things here." He hung up.

I needed to call Jenna to see what she had heard. She would be at work, but glancing at my watch, most likely on her lunch break. She answered on the first ring. "I know why you're calling, John. I've heard from my mother and my father, and had to explain things to half a dozen people at work this morning. This is so very embarrassing. They've heard a rumor, something about dead bodies and the Dawson pond, and this being a small town and only one Dawson family here, it doesn't take them too long to figure out I might, or maybe should, know something. And nobody has talked with me about what the crime lab has found. It seems like...." She stopped suddenly. "Look, I'm eating lunch now. Let's talk later." She hung up.

The one member of the Dawson family I had not talked with was Nate. I was considering calling him when my phone rang. It was the Dawson home number again, leading me to think Mrs. Dawson was calling back to apologize for hanging up on me. Instead, it was her husband. "Listen here, John, this whole business has gotten out of hand. I just talked with the Marsh fellow—what do they call them?—Special Agent Marsh. He tried to tell me what's going on at the pond, but I'm here at the house with Martha, and she's been getting calls all morning from anybody and everybody about dead bodies in our pond and no one's had the damned courtesy to keep us informed and...."

"Hold on," I said to Nate, speaking more firmly than I should for someone dating his daughter. "Pete Marsh was trying to reach you this morning, but your home line was busy. All this is not his fault and I know it's not your fault. It is what it is. Pete and everyone else out there at the pond are just doing their jobs. The whole thing appears to be a tragedy, a series of murders that took place over several years. I have no idea how the information got leaked, but it would have become public knowledge at some point before too long. Pete said the GBI is planning to ask anyone with possible knowledge of the case to call their tip hotline." I paused, waiting for Nate to say more. He remained silent. "But if you back off a minute and think about it, the investigation is in its early stages. There's a lot they haven't figured out, but probably will at some point. Like the identity of the bodies—the victims, if that's the right word. Sooner or later the cops are going to know who they are. Maybe DNA, or maybe something else will give the answer. And when they do, they'll start working on how and why that person disappeared, because surely that's what happened. If you assume that one person is responsible for these deaths, pretty soon they will be closing in on the killer. The case will be solved, and things can return to normal."

Nate said nothing for a long moment, then, "You make it all sound so simple and easy, don't you?" The line went dead. I stared at the phone screen for a long minute, realizing that in the course of an hour, all three members of the Dawson family had hung up on me.

CHAPTER 11

The Dawsons were angry. There was no other way to describe it, though I imagined they might try to find other words. They were angry that their peaceful life was being torn apart by the discoveries at the family pond, that the situation was beyond their control, and that they had become subjects of groundless suspicion. Having nowhere else to direct their fears and resentment, and no one else to blame, they aimed them squarely at me. I wasn't sure what to do. My greatest fear was the loss of Jenna, but my sole sin appeared to be my role as the bearer of bad news in the form of a randomly discovered shoe filled with human bones. I decided my best response was to back off, let everything take its course and see what would happen. If Jenna truly loved me as she had said so many times, she would call. The investigation would certainly absolve Nate and Martha Dawson, and maybe, just maybe, we could all pick up the pieces and move ahead with our lives in the same direction as before.

The remainder of the week seemed to pass quickly. I heard nothing from the Dawsons, Pete Marsh or Jenna. Several times I picked up the phone to call her, but was determined to let her make the next move. To my surprise, it appeared that the news of the discoveries was not immediately reported either online or on broadcast media. I found out from Pete later that the GBI had convinced the various media outlets to sit on what they knew, promising to give them full access to the story once the investigation was further along. That would come when the investigators felt they had enough to ask for the public's help.

Late Friday afternoon Pete called with an update. "I believe the lab has made some progress this week. On Victim A, the youngest of the four and the body that appears to have been there the longest, they've managed to extract some usable DNA from the interior of a tooth and are working on that. Don't know where it will lead. But, the two most workable findings are the Nike athletic shoes and blue shirt he was wearing. The shoes appear to be basically new—they have very little wear on the soles. Assuming they were purchased shortly before his death, that puts the date roughly twelve years ago. That will help narrow the search. And the real kicker is the polyester polo shirt. It had a Georgia Southern logo embroidered on it. The lab tells me that based on his assumed age he could well have been a student there. But the downside is that the school has something like 25,000 students enrolled at any time in dozens of programs, and you know with that number you're going to have quite a few transferring, dropping out, quitting or whatever. It's a help, but there's still so much work to be done."

"That's great," I said. "A start at least."

"Hope so, and by the way, didn't your friend Jenna go to school at Southern?"

"She did. How did you know that? I didn't know you'd interviewed her."

"We haven't. Just doing the public record check. She's got a long history, but I guess you know that?" Pete's tone was neutral.

"Yeah, a lot of us do...," I replied.

"Touché. I wasn't trying to make a point, John, just letting you know. Neither she nor her parents are suspects at this point, and there's no reason to think that will change. But in this kind of investigation, you've got to go where the evidence leads you, no matter what or who."

"I understand."

"Oh, and on the victim with the engraved wedding ring,

we're searching marriage databases across the southeast trying to match the date and initials with names. No luck there as yet. The lab guys haven't been able to retrieve any good DNA thus far from his remains, or those of the other two."

"Good," I replied. I wasn't in a mood to ask questions.

"And one more thing. It's early in the investigation, so we've been meeting twice weekly to go over where we are, plus a little brainstorming about what we should be focusing on. Someone brought up the obvious fact that whoever dumped the bodies needed a boat to get them out in open water. It had to be big enough to hold the killer—assuming we're talking about a single individual—plus the corpse and the chain or blocks or whatever was used to weigh it down in the water. It wasn't like someone could just pull up, take the victim out of the trunk of his—or her—car and wade out to get to the deepest point of the lake. Whoever dumped them had to know where that deepest point was. Now, Nate Dawson told us that flat-bottomed fishing boat had been there for many years, chained to that tree, but with the key available if you knew where to look for it. So, based on that logic, whoever dumped them had to be familiar with the pond and the boat and where to find the key." Pete waited for my response. I couldn't tell if the "or her" comment was aimed at Jenna—or Mrs. Dawson.

"True, and that's a great observation. But I'm sure the Dawsons told you they'd had church picnics and family gatherings and even Jenna's wedding there."

"They did," Pete said, "and as we speak, Agent Hodges, who's working with us on this, is going to be interviewing all three of them to get a list of folks who had visited the pond over the years and might know about the gate lock combination and boat key hiding place."

If the Dawsons were not already angry enough, I thought,

this would surely push them over the edge. "That's probably going to be a long list," I said. "And you'll be likely to upset a whole bunch of people when you start interviewing elderly grandmothers about the details of what they did at those church picnics."

Pete laughed. "We're not planning on interviewing anyone other than the Dawsons at this point. Just want to get the information in case it might fit in later as the investigation progresses. I can't see those 'elderly grandmothers' confessing to skinny-dipping."

Not having spoken with Jenna, I began to feel like the walls were closing in on me. There was a wholesale art event scheduled for the weekend at one of the downtown convention centers in Atlanta. I had not planned to attend but reasoned that a change of location might improve my mood. Making the excuse that the gallery could use some lower-priced inventory, I booked a last-minute room for Saturday night at a hotel in Buckhead. I intended to leave Savannah at 6:00 a.m. to arrive for the show's opening at 10:00. I packed a few things in a small suitcase and went to bed early.

Around eleven, I was awakened by the persistent buzzing of my cell. Fumbling in the darkness, I picked it up to see Jenna's number on the display. "Hey," she said. "I hope you don't mind my calling so late."

"No, it's fine. I went to bed early because I'm getting up a little after five tomorrow morning. I'm going to Atlanta for a trade show." There was silence on the other end of the line. I continued, "I haven't heard from you all week."

"I know, and I'm sorry. Just so much going on. I talked with Mr. Marsh, the GBI agent. I want to see you."

"I'll be back late Sunday afternoon. I could swing through Claxton on my way and...."

"No, sooner. Like tomorrow."

"Jenna, I've made plans, and have already paid for entry to the show and booked a room…."

"Can I go with you? I miss you and want to tell you in person how miserable I feel about the way I've been acting."

My first reaction was to say, "Yes, yes, and yes!" but instead I asked, "I'd like to see you, of course, but can it wait?"

"I don't want to wait. I need to talk with you soon. I'm worried. I want your advice." Knowing Jenna as well as I did, I thought I detected a sense of fright.

"Why don't you come to Atlanta with me? Is Robert there? You could…."

"No, he's at my parents for the weekend. You can pick me up here in Claxton early tomorrow and I'll ride with you. It'll only add about fifteen minutes to your drive."

I was torn. I wanted to see Jenna, the Jenna that I thought I knew, the one person I could be at ease with and bare my soul to. But something seemed to have changed with the discoveries at the Dawson pond. And what did her speaking with Pete Marsh have to do with things? He'd told me that the GBI planned to interview Jenna and her parents. Was that why she called? There was only one way to find out. No matter what the outcome between the two of us, I felt as if I had nothing to lose by taking her with me. I said, "Sure, I'll pick you up at your place about 6:30 tomorrow morning."

CHAPTER 12

As I arrived the next morning, Jenna was waiting for me on the front stoop of her apartment, carrying only a small suitcase, shivering slightly in the cool morning air and twilight of dawn. She hopped in the car, gave me a quick smooch, and settled in with a few trivial questions: "Did you sleep well?" "How long do you think it will take us to get to Atlanta?" and the like. She had said on the phone the night before that she was "worried" and "needed to talk" with me. It was clear that she was avoiding my asking the most obvious question, "Why?" I didn't push things, trying to give her a chance to relax. We were on the interstate when she finally said, "I told you Pete Marsh called last night."

"You did. And…?" I waited for her answer.

"He was very polite, said that one of the agents, a man named Hodges, would be contacting me and my parents to interview us sometime in the next week or two. That was fine. And then he asked, 'Didn't you attend college at Georgia Southern in Statesboro?' I said I did, but he wanted to know the exact years I was there, and if I participated in any extracurricular things, like sororities or clubs, or was I involved in school-sponsored sports such as tennis or golf. It was all so strange. I felt like he was fishing for the right answer, looking to connect something from my college days with something else. I mean, he was cordial and all, but his questions were very specific about things I might have done or been involved in before I got married."

"Why does that worry you?"

"I don't know," Jenna said, sighing. "It just seems like everyone, those people who've called my parents, the ones at work, all of them seem to think that since we—my family that is—have a private pond, we must somehow know or be connected to whoever committed those terrible crimes. It's like you read about the police grilling a suspect for hours and hours until he just gives up and confesses, even if he's innocent." She reached over and touched my arm. "John, there's nothing there. I haven't done anything. My parents haven't done anything. Please believe me."

Taking my eyes off the road for a brief moment, I looked at her and said, "Why would I not believe you?" She did not respond, instead gripping my arm ever more tightly. I was sorely tempted to tell her about the crime lab's findings on Victim A, the fact that his age and the shirt he was wearing suggested, but with no other verification, that he might have been a student at Georgia Southern around the time she was in school there. To do so, though, would only have made matters worse. I changed the subject, asking Jenna if she'd like to go out to dinner after we finished at the art sale event. She smiled and said she would, leaving things unsettled. It bothered me that both Jenna and her father were troubled at the prospect of being interviewed by the investigators.

The rest of the trip went smoothly. Jenna attended the show with me, helping choose some colorful but inexpensive original artworks to cater to tourists wanting to take back something to remember their visit to Savannah. I had learned to cheerfully offer free shipping to the buyers' homes, a cost that had already been considered when setting the asking price. We had breakfast delivered by room service Sunday morning, which included a newspaper, an increasingly rare form of communication in the digital age. Flipping through the pages, Jenna commented it was strange that she had not seen the discovery of the bodies reported in the usual news outlets.

"I believe they are waiting for the crime lab to complete the basics of analyzing what they've found, then they'll most likely ask for input from the public. They'll limit what they reveal to things that won't have a negative impact on the investigation or on any criminal cases if they ever identify the person or people responsible for the murders. Right now they don't have a lot to go on, other than the remains of four unidentified dead bodies. They'll set up a special tip line for people to call." Jenna frowned but said nothing.

We left Atlanta before noon, arriving back in Claxton shortly after three o'clock. Jenna suggested that instead of taking her home, we go by her parents' house to pick up Robert. I agreed, thinking it might give me a chance to see if the Dawsons were still upset with me. I hadn't spoken to either one since they abruptly ended our phone conversations. Somewhat to my surprise, they were pleasant, inviting me in for a visit. The pond was not mentioned. I felt better. Robert, who seemed to have recovered from the trauma of the shoe discovery, begged to spend another night with his grandparents as one of his school friends was coming over for supper. Jenna agreed before we left, headed for her house. As we were pulling out of the Dawsons' driveway, she said, out of the blue, "Let's go to the pond."

I looked at her. "Are you serious?"

"I am. I haven't seen it since the day you took Robert fishing, since that day you found the…." She didn't finish the sentence.

"Isn't the crime lab crew still working there?"

"No, my dad called late Friday afternoon to say that they've finished and cleared out. He said they put the old combination lock back on the gate."

"Why do you want to visit? You've been so upset about all

that's gone on."

"I know I have, but I just want to." She gazed out the window at the forest landscape zipping past. "The pond..., it's just been so much a part of my life. I played there when I was half Robert's age. My friends and I went swimming there when I was in high school and college. And the wedding.... I know it all went bad, but it meant so very much to me at the time. I just want to see it."

Twenty minutes later we arrived at the locked gate on the dirt road. Jenna hopped out, undid the lock, removed the chain and swung the gate widely open. The former dirt track now seemed like a highway, with multiple truckloads of gravel filling its former ruts. The grass of the rustic pasture space now lay beaten down by the weeks-long comings and goings of police and investigators. The pond that once reflected the forest and the sky was now little more than a large muddy hole, still mostly dry after being drained of its water. I parked where the crime lab vans had been as we both surveyed the devastation. Jenna began crying. "It will never be the same," she sobbed softly.

"Time will heal," I said, trying to comfort her. "A few good rains and the pond will be full again. The grass will regrow, and the gravel in the road will only make it easier for you and me—and Robert—to have picnics, and fish, and...."

"No, it's all lost," she interrupted. "It will never be the same." For a long moment she looked about, then said, "Let's go home." It was clear that something very special to Jenna had been lost. I felt so sorry for her, but there was little I could do. I dropped her off at her apartment. She did not invite me in, but said she'd call in "a day or so." I had no idea what that meant, and no idea of my place in her current or future life.

I brooded about the past two days on my way back to

Savannah. I still did not have a good understanding—or would "feeling" be the right word?—for the reasons and emotions behind the Dawsons' reactions. Even if I totally understood everything, there was little or nothing I could do to change things. The one positive thing was reflected in what I had said to Jenna: time will pass, the rains will come, the grass will grow back, the pond will once again be full. But where did I fit in all of that?

I had just settled in at my office in the gallery on Monday morning when Pete Marsh called. "Hey, John, hope you had a good weekend. A lot's gone on since we last spoke, and I wanted to bring you up to date. It looks like we're finally making progress. But before I say any more, I want you to promise me that you'll keep this confidential, especially from the Dawsons, at least until we have the opportunity to interview them. It probably wouldn't matter at all, but when we start asking questions, I don't want any advance knowledge of what we've found to shape in any way the answers that we get."

CHAPTER 13

"There's a lot, so where do I start?" Pete began. "The reason I'm telling you this is that the Dawsons are looking to you for advice. They see—and rightfully so—this whole thing, the investigation, the intrusion into their lives, as something negative, an invasion of their privacy. I've been doing this a long time, John. I've seen plenty of cases where important witnesses would not cooperate just because they felt maybe the investigators had some agenda, were trying to pin some crime on them, or somehow involve them when they knew they were totally innocent. I see the potential for that here. We need—we have to have—their active support if we're going to solve these murders. And they need someone besides us, someone they trust, to reinforce that. They're looking to you, so we all need your help."

Pete was correct. Without the active assistance of the Dawsons, discovering who dumped the bodies would be all the more difficult. Only they knew who had been at the pond, or the identities of those who had potential access. I said I would back him up, not worried that I was in any way betraying my loyalty to Jenna or her parents.

"Okay, then, let me get started. First, with Victim A, the young man with the tennis shoes and Georgia Southern polo shirt. The good news is that the lab was finally able to get a good, clean DNA profile on him. But the disappointing news is that they couldn't match it to any of the national forensic DNA databases. That probably doesn't mean a lot, since he was young and had never been in trouble with the law. But it's going to be a godsend once we start asking for the public's input and assistance. I believe we should be able to make a quick

ID once we set up the hotline and spread the word.

"About Victims B and C, I'm sorry to say there's not a lot more. The only finding of possible help is the fact that C was apparently fully clothed when his body was dumped in the pond. Most of his clothing had rotted away, but he appeared to be wearing a leather belt with a fancy buckle that survived the years on the pond's bottom, plus what appear to be some expensive cowboy-style alligator boots. The belt buckle was big, about two inches by three inches, and appears to be handmade of sterling silver. Those are the kind of unique findings that should help us make an ID. And the older guy with the engraved wedding ring, Victim D, nothing on that as yet. It's nearly impossible to track down wedding registrations, compare them with dates, and so on. The lab folks say it's a waste of time—the guy could have gotten married in Las Vegas, or Timbuktu. Again, though, that will be a positive for a confirmation if we come up with a potential name."

"That's some progress," I said, "but nothing too definite."

"No, and I forgot to mention that the crime lab is working on creating an image of what the victims might have looked like based on their facial bone structure. The new thing is to feed three-dimensional CT scans of the skull into a graphics program with an AI component—artificial intelligence. The computer produces a new 3D digital rendering of how the skull, and face in particular, might have looked in life, and the artist works with that to come up with a realistic drawing. It's one of those technological marvels—sounds great, but understanding exactly how it works is beyond my pay grade."

"Interesting."

"Yes, and it's made a difference in a number of tough ID cases around the nation. We're just getting into the technique here in Georgia."

"So what's the next step?" I asked.

"The interviews. We want to interview each person separately—that's standard practice, but I guess you know that. Not sure it's necessary in this case, but sometimes you get a red flag, two totally different stories from people who should be singing from the same sheet of music." I liked Pete's expression.

"Jenna said that someone named Hodges was doing the interviews, is that still correct?"

"For sure. Randy Hodges is the best we've got. Sort of innocent looking, asking sometimes what seem like dumb questions, but he's sharp as a tack. Never lets whoever he's interviewing know he's on to something, but just keeps picking away. He's a nice fellow. I guess you'll get to meet him if you're sitting in on the interviews. The Dawsons, at least the parents, said you would be there as their 'advisor' during the process."

It had never occurred to me that they actually wanted me to be physically there. I had assumed I might be doing some telephonic hand-holding, but had no intention of being anyone's legal bodyguard. I said nothing about this to Pete, but instead asked, "When is the first interview?"

"Tomorrow. Didn't Mr. Dawson tell you? He said you'd be there 'to keep me out of trouble.'"

"Uh…, no. He hasn't said anything. Can we maybe put this off?"

I couldn't see Pete's face on the other end of the line, but I imagined he was frowning. "Not really," he said. "We've spent a number of weeks getting to this point, and I don't think anyone at the Bureau wants more delays. I'm getting a little pressure from on high. They want to see 'more progress.' That was the exact term from Nelson Jackson, my boss, the guy I report to. You met him briefly at the pond." Pete paused, evidently deciding what to say next. "Look, John, I'm sorry this is such a rush, and particularly sorry Nate Dawson didn't notify you. But I'm kinda under the gun here. I haven't been with the GBI all that long, and while I've been very busy with homicide investigations, this is my first big case. Putting off this interview would look bad, and at this point I really don't need that."

I could understand Pete's reasoning. I realized he was politely trying to say, "That's your problem, not mine." I smiled for no one's benefit and said, "I'll change my plans and make it happen. Where is the interview?"

"At the Evans County Sheriff's Department, behind the courthouse in Claxton. We'll keep this first interview as low key as possible. Just Randy Hodges and his voice recorder. Are you okay with that?"

"Sure, no problem," I lied once again. We casually ended the conversation and hung up.

I checked with Jessica, asking her to clear my schedule for the next couple of days as I had to be in Claxton to attend to some business. She agreed, rolling her eyes and murmuring that Jenna would be upset if I kept referring to her as "some business." I pretended not to hear.

The next morning at 9:45 I was sitting in the same interview room where Sheriff Hearn and I discussed my discovery of the bone-filled shoe weeks before. He stuck his head in briefly to say hello, followed soon after by Nate Dawson who was ushered into the room by a receptionist. "The GBI agent called and said he was running a little behind, but will be here in about ten minutes," she said. Nate Dawson shook my hand without speaking, then settled into a chair, still silent. He looked like he was about to cry.

"Are you okay?" I asked.

He nodded without answering, taking out a handkerchief to blow his nose. After a long moment without words, he looked at me and said, "I never in all the world thought it would come to this. All these years I've been struggling to make a good home for my wife and my daughter, to provide for their needs and now...." He didn't finish the sentence.

"I'm so sorry," I said. "I know this is stressful, but it will work out. We'll get past this and...."

He turned and looked at me sharply. "We...?"

At just that moment the door opened as the receptionist showed in a man appearing to be no older than his mid-thirties. He was neatly dressed in khaki and wearing a long-sleeved shirt bearing an embroidered GBI logo. "I'm Randolph Hodges," he said, smiling and extending his hand to Nate Dawson. "You must be Mr. Dawson, the owner of the pond?" Turning to me, "And you're John O'Toole? Pete Marsh speaks well of you."

After a moment of introductions and small talk, the agent placed a digital recorder in the middle of the table, pressed a button, and began, "I presume we all know why we're here. This is an informal interview, Mr. Dawson. I'm not going to ask you to give a sworn statement, but I will be recording everything we say simply to help me keep up with it. I'm here representing the Georgia Bureau of Investigation, and we need your help in solving these apparent murders and the dumping of the victims' bodies in your pond. To make it clear at the outset, neither you nor your family are suspects in the investigation at this point, but we are obligated to ask you to tell us anything and everything you know that might have any bearing on the case."

Hodges waited for Nate's response. Nate stared at him, saying nothing. I wondered why Hodges chose to use the phrase, "at this point."

CHAPTER 14

Nate Dawson stared back silently at Agent Hodges, his arms crossed in front of his chest, unconsciously signaling his displeasure at the situation he found himself in. After a moment of silence he said, "It's my wife's pond; it ain't mine. She inherited it."

"Okay, then," Hodges said pleasantly, "Sorry for the mistake." Sensing Nate's hostility, he continued, "Mr. Dawson, in case I wasn't clear, this is not a deposition or a legal proceeding. It's really just a get-acquainted interview. I'm sure we would both agree that whoever put those bodies in your family's pond needs to be identified and, if appropriate, charged with the crimes. That will clear your names and reputations. Until that happens, this whole thing is going to be hanging over your heads." He waited for Nate's response.

Taking a deep breath, Nate unfolded his arms, glanced at me and then said, "I guess you're right, Mr. Hodges. It's just that this is something I didn't sign up for. So, let's get started and get it over with."

Hodges flashed a quick smile and looked at his notes. "Tell me about yourself," he asked. A totally open-ended question if there ever was one, I thought.

"Well," Nate began, "I've lived here in Claxton pretty much all my life except for four years off in the army—I was kind of a wild one back in the day. Got in a bit of trouble here and the judge suggested signing up might be a good thing. Martha and I have been married about thirty-three or thirty-four years, I think that's about right, and we have one daughter, Jenna, who's friends with Mr. O'Toole here. Woulda had more kids but the doctor said that's not gonna happen. I work here at McKinsey Forest Products, that's a wood chip mill, turns mostly pine trees into chips which are then shipped out by rail to make paper and cardboard boxes, that sorta thing. Been there more than twenty years. I'm a shift supervisor. My wife don't work now. She did one time when they had a sewing factory here, but that closed down. I make enough for us to get by, not a lot more."

Although I doubted if Nate noticed it, Hodges eyed him intensely as he spoke, appearing to take in every detail of his voice, his inflections, his body language. "Sounds like you've had a good life."

"We get by," Nate said, now seeming more relaxed.

"Tell me more about your job," Hodges asked. "You said you'd been there for a good while. How long have you been a supervisor? I guess that was a good bump in your pay?"

"Oh, I don't know, about ten years or so. I'm thinking it was right after Jenna got married...," quickly adding, "...for the first time. She's divorced now."

"Pays better, I'd guess?" Hodges asked.

"A good bit, yeah, but there's a lot that can go wrong in that type of operation, and the shift supervisor is the one in charge. You earn your money."

"Do you drink?" It seemed to me an odd question.

"No. Well, a beer every now and then. Can't really afford to drink and work."

"Tell me about joining the army," Hodges said.

It was a loaded question, but Nate had mentioned it first, making it fair game for the interview. He frowned and began, "You know how it is when you're pushing twenty years old. Think you can conquer the world. It happened one night, I got to drinking too much. I guess you could say I was good and drunk. I had a girlfriend then, a cute little blond thing, and we was at a dance. This guy from Statesboro—he was a student up there at the college—is in town, and he starts hitting on her real hard. Got me upset, and I started hitting on him real hard, but in another way. He ended up in the hospital, broken bones and all. I ended up in jail. Anyway, I got this lawyer, and when I came before the judge, they talked it out that if I agreed to sign up for the military, things would stop right there. 'Cause if I didn't, I was looking at a couple of years in jail. So I signed up, changed my ways, and when I came back home I settled down, met Martha, got married and started a family." He paused. "That enough, or you want to hear more?" The whole episode was something he was clearly ashamed of.

"That's enough. It was good you got your life turned around." The conversation between Nate and Agent Hodges, now more relaxed, went on for the next hour and a half. The questions were for the most part banal and benign, focusing on who, other than family members, had visited or had access to the Dawson pond over the past decade. Nate made it clear he had no idea who might be responsible. He said he and his wife occasionally went fishing there, and mentioned church events and Jenna's wedding without going into detail. It seemed a bit strange to me that Hodges didn't ask follow-up questions about those events. All the while the agent appeared to be listening intently, occasionally scribbling notes on a small legal pad. I remained silent. It had soon become clear that other than moral support, my presence was not required.

Apparently having run out of questions, Hodges said, "Well, Mr. Dawson, I believe that's all I wanted to ask you. We really appreciate your cooperation and assistance. This case, these apparent murders, are terrible things, and your family's support means so much to everyone." They stood up and shook hands heartily. "I think we will want to interview your wife sometime soon, maybe this week, if possible?"

Nate hesitated, then said, "My wife wanted me to tell you that she's not gonna talk with you. She didn't want to be hassled and embarrassed and whatever.... But I tell you, Mr. Hodges, you seem like a good guy, and when you think about it, you are right that it's in everyone's best interest to get this all behind us. So, I'm gonna talk with her as soon as I get to the house. I think I can convince her. She's gonna want me here, but you said you wanted to interview us separately and I don't need to miss no more work than I have 'cause of this, so I'll ask John here if he will sit in to keep her company. That okay?"

"Sure."

"When you want to see her? Maybe tomorrow? Let's get this stuff over with." Nate now seemed positive about being interviewed. Hodges handed Nate his business card, instructing him to call him as soon as possible after speaking with his wife. Everyone left, with Nate telling me he would be in touch as soon as he spoke to Martha. I was a little annoyed that he had not asked me if the following day would be convenient. But then, my goal was to marry his daughter, and if this was one of those necessary things, I would do my best to comply. It had been days since I'd spoken with Jenna.

I had been back in Savannah about half an hour when Nate called to say that he had spoken with both his wife and the GBI agent. The interview was scheduled the next day for 2:00 p.m. in the same location. I said I would be there.

Martha Dawson and I both pulled into parking spaces in front of the Evans County Sheriff's Department at almost the same time, nearly half an hour before the scheduled interview. She saw me, waved and flashed a brief smile. I was expecting, or better hoping, that Jenna would be with her, but she arrived alone. We exchanged a few pleasantries, walked into the office together and were shown to the small conference room with its video cameras peering down on us. I assumed that these conferences were being recorded on video. "I do not want to be here, John. You know that," she said.

"I do. Mr. Dawson told me."

"But he said Agent Hodges is a good guy, and wants as much as we do to see these crimes solved, so I agreed to let him interview me. If he starts anything now, yelling at me or trying to make me say things, you're going to protect me, right?"

"Yes, of course, but I don't think you'll need to worry about any of that."

Hodges walked in the door just as I was finishing my sentence. "You must be Mrs. Dawson," he said cordially. "I'm Randy Hodges, and I'm an investigator with the Georgia Bureau of Investigation." I noticed that he seemed more relaxed and informal than the preceding day, introducing himself this time as "Randy" instead of the more proper "Randolph." "I enjoyed getting to meet your husband yesterday. He seems like a fine man and spoke so highly of you," Hodges continued, something that I did not at all recall happening. This guy is good, I thought. Following the previous day's pattern, Mrs. Dawson and Hodges chatted for the next few minutes, each seemingly scoping the other out.

Getting to the actual interview, Hodges focused on the pond, how long it had been in Mrs. Dawson's family, from whom she inherited it, and whether or not other relatives might have access. He asked about the church picnics, with Mrs. Dawson promising to give him the name of the church pastor as a source of more information. "Now, Mr. Dawson says you formerly worked in a sewing factory here, is that correct?"

“Yes, but it shut down. All the jobs got moved to Mexico and Vietnam and places like that. You can’t buy any American-made clothing these days.”

“I guess that hurt you financially?”

“Oh, my lord, yes. We didn’t know how we were going to make it. It was all we could do to scrape by on what both Nate and I made, and then we were trying to help out our daughter, Jenna, too, and it was just….”

“Was that about the time Mr. Dawson got a promotion?” Hodges asked.

“Yes, thank Jesus. He was doing swing shift work—twelve-hour shifts either night or day, and then this position comes open and he gets promoted. It was our salvation.”

“I know that’s a stroke of good luck,” Hodges said, scribbling a note on his legal pad.

“No, we prayed over it. It was an answer to our prayers.”

“Of course. The Lord moves in mysterious ways,” Hodges said, solemnly.

“Yes. Romans 11:33: ‘How unsearchable are his judgments and how inscrutable his ways!’” Mrs. Dawson replied, correcting him.

CHAPTER 15

I assumed Jenna would be asked to give an interview, but had no idea when or whether or not she wanted me present. That changed the next morning when she called me from work, obviously upset, saying she had just gotten a call "from the police wanting to talk with me about what happened at the pond." After getting her to calm down a bit by voicing my support and reassurance, it turned out that Randy Hodges, the GBI agent, had called and asked if she were available for an interview sometime in the next few days. Jenna said she knew her parents had been interviewed by the GBI—not the "police" as she said—and that things went well, without going into detail. I suggested she call them. She hung up, saying she would. I had hoped she would say she missed me and offer some excuse, however lame, about why she had not called me before. She did not.

An hour later Jenna called back, this time sounding more like her usual self. She had spoken with both her mother and father who described the interviews as a necessary if annoying waste of time, but not intimidating or traumatic. Both said Agent Hodges was courteous and polite. She scheduled her interview at the Evans County Sheriff's Department for the following Monday afternoon and wanted to know if I could be there to support her. "Both my mom and dad said you were great. They couldn't have done it without you, so I want you there, I need you there." I did not want to explain to her that I had done little more than sit in a chair and listen to the conversation, but Jenna's use of the words "want you" and "need you" would probably have prompted me to accompany her on a tour of Hell if she had asked.

I gently reminded Jenna that we had not talked in a few days, suggesting that we might spend some time together over the coming weekend. "I can give you a few pointers before the interview on Monday." She said that sounded good, but she planned to have Robert for the weekend and needed to spend some "mama time" with him. She said they might go to Savannah for the day. I told her to call me if she had any questions, but otherwise I would meet her a little before 2:00 p.m. at the sheriff's office. By the time I left for Claxton on Monday, I had heard nothing from her.

I was curious about one important thing. Pete Marsh had filled me in on some of the things the crime lab had discovered about the remains of the four bodies found in the pond. Based on what he said, Victim A might well have been a student from Georgia Southern, and if the suppositions about his age were correct, he probably was there at or near the time Jenna was also enrolled. But Pete had only given me an overview, and in the process made me promise to keep the information confidential. As much as I cared about Jenna, I could not break that promise by revealing anything to her. So far as I knew, these details were still confidential and would probably remain so unless the GBI followed through with the plans to ask for the public's help in identifying the victims. Randy Hodges was certainly aware of the lab's findings. I was curious to see how the potential Georgia Southern connection would play out in his interview with Jenna.

Monday turned out to be a balmy day with clear skies. I was sitting on a bench outside the sheriff's office when Jenna arrived just in time for the interview. She smiled when she saw me, and rushed over to give me a hug before entering the building. "I've missed you," she said.

"I know. It's been too long since we've been together, or

even talked."

"That's my fault. This whole..., whole thing, has been terrible. I wake up in the middle of the night terrified about what might come of it. I mean, is someone we know the murderer? How did they know to get to the pond, and why would they dump the bodies there? Were they trying to send some sort of a message? I don't think my parents have any enemies, but I did find out that my daddy got in trouble one time and had to join the army to keep out of jail. But he's always been the kindest, sweetest man and...." She was interrupted by the receptionist standing at the door of the building and waving that it was time to start the interview.

Agent Hodges was waiting for us in the interview room. He was friendly but professional, and as before chatted with Jenna, each of them assessing the other. He assured her this was an informal interview seeking further paths of investigation about how and why the victims were secreted in the Dawson pond. Jenna seemed relaxed and cooperative. They talked briefly about her past, the fact that she had been married and was now divorced, and her current job at a small manufacturing firm. I was certain Hodges was aware of her history of drug abuse and run-ins with the law, but he did not mention it at that point. The discussion next turned to Jenna's education. "Agent Marsh mentioned that you attended college at Georgia Southern in Statesboro," he said. "Tell me a bit about your time there." Another open-ended question.

Jenna smiled. "I guess I was kind of a country girl moved to the city. Growing up in Claxton, life was a lot slower. I loved being at Southern, and met a lot of great people there. A few of them became lifelong friends. Nothing really dramatic happened, though, not then anyway."

"And I understand you got married right out of college, is

that right?"

"Yes, I married Carl McClure. Rates up there as one of the biggest mistakes of my life, but the good thing is that we had a son, Robert Carlton McClure, Jr., who has been the main source of happiness in my life for all of his nine and a half years." She glanced quicky at me and winked. "I guess you know we've been divorced for a good while now."

"Yes, I saw that in the case notes. Did you meet Carl there at school? Did you date anyone else?" I wondered where Hodges was going with this.

"Well, you know how it is. I guess I had quite a few 'dates' but nothing really serious until I met Carl. He was planning to be a lawyer. That didn't happen. I guess we got married because I was finishing college and it was what you were supposed to do...."

"Did you have any other serious boyfriends, serious relationships?"

"Not really. There was one time though when Carl and I split up over something silly. I think I saw him with another girl and accused him of cheating, or something like that. I had a few dates and started going out with another guy named Billy. I hate to say it, but I forget his last name—I think it was Thomas or Thompson or something like that...."

"Would you say that was a serious relationship?" Hodges asked.

Jenna thought a moment before replying, "Well, we made it past the third date, if that's what you're asking...." She did not look at me this time.

"Gotcha," Hodges said, pretending to study his notes. "So why did you break up? And how did you get back with Carl?"

"I honestly don't remember. Maybe I decided that Carl was The One after all. You know how it is at that age."

Hodges smiled and nodded. I was thinking this line of questioning had to be related to Victim A, though Jenna had no way of knowing that.

"I understand from your parents that when you were in high school and college you would sometimes have friends out to the pond to..., what?"

"To visit, or fish, or lay in the sun, or drink beer—we were mostly underage at that point in our lives. I'd let my parents know we'd be at the pond, but they never came out or bothered us."

"Did any of you ever go out in the boat that your daddy keeps there?"

Jenna wrinkled her brow. "Yes, just about every time. But how did you know about the boat?"

"I was there with the crime lab guys several times. Just curious." It was an evasive answer, but I knew what he was thinking.

After several more questions, Hodges said, "I understand you once had a problem with substance abuse, methamphetamine specifically, that you worked in a 'gentleman's club,' and that you had some run-ins with the law. Do you think anyone or anything associated with that part of your life might be related to the bodies?"

It was a tough question, but a necessary one. Jenna blanched, looked down, then back at the agent. "That whole part of my life was one of those crazy things, a time that I wished had never happened, something I wish I could erase from my past, from my memory and from everyone else's memory. I'm ashamed of it. And to be honest, I knew you would ask about that, and worried about what I would say. To answer your question, yes, I was around some pretty bad people. Druggies, misfits, cheating husbands, liars, criminal types.

I wasn't directly involved in anything, but I can't say I didn't know about it, or know it existed. It was just part of the game. But since that day when my precious Robert snagged that shoe in the water, I've tried to think if there was a link one way or another to things in my past, and I just can't find one. So again, yes, there may be a possible connection, but no, I don't know of it if it exists." Tears were trickling down her cheeks. I reached over and handed her a tissue.

CHAPTER 16

The silence of the small room was broken only by Jenna's sobs. I reached out to take her hand, but she slipped it away. Agent Hodges stared at his notes as the unblinking eyes of the video cameras stared down at the three of us from above. After a moment, he said, "I'm sorry, Jenna. I know this is a lot, dragging up old memories. I understand how you must feel." Jenna continued to stare at the table, dabbing at her eyes. "But please remember," he continued, "what happens today in this room is confidential." I remained silent, skeptical of the longevity of that promise.

After a moment or two Jenna asked, "Is that all for today? Are you finished? I don't know if I can go on like this."

"I understand," Hodges said. "You've been very helpful and I appreciate that. Why don't we call it a day for now? I'm not sure we'll need to talk with you again, but if we do I hope it won't be as upsetting." Jenna nodded, not replying.

Hodges rose, thanked us both for our assistance and said he was headed back toward Savannah. He said he would contact Jenna if he had any follow-up questions. With that he shut the door, leaving Jenna and me alone together for the first time in what seemed like weeks. "I'm sorry," I said, echoing Hodges's words. I didn't know what else to say. This time Jenna reached out and took my hand.

"Why did he want to know about my time at Southern?" she asked. "And who I was dating? Does the fact my friends came and visited at the pond more than ten years ago make me a suspect, or what? And Billy—I wish I could remember his last name—is he a suspect, too, just because we dated for a few months? I just don't understand how...." She broke into tears once more, not finishing her sentence.

"Look, let me take you home. I'll stay there until you are feeling better. I love you."

Jenna raised her head and looked at me through tear-stained eyes. "I would like to say I love you as well, but somehow I don't feel worthy of that, or anything really. I try so hard, and I seem to fail at everything I want to do."

I drove Jenna home in her car, leaving my aging Lincoln at the sheriff's office. I showed her to the door, hoping she would ask me to stay. Instead, she said she wanted to, needed to be alone. It was only a ten-minute or so walk to where my car was parked. I said the fresh air would do me good, gave her a hug and set out toward the courthouse and sheriff's office.

The walk gave me a chance to think. Jenna had every right to be ashamed and upset. Just when her life seemed to be on an even keel, this storm of forced memories had opened old wounds, old embarrassments, old insecurities. She couldn't change the past no matter what, but living with it made her life all the more difficult. I only wished that she would let me be more supportive.

I was back in my apartment at the gallery by late afternoon and seriously considering having a glass of bourbon when Pete Marsh called. "Hey, John, I spoke with Randy Hodges about his interviews with the Dawsons. He said they went well overall. Didn't learn much from the parents, but he wants to interview Jenna again at some point. She apparently got all teary-eyed once he started asking about her past."

"That's true, but look Pete, as I said before a lot of us have a past we're not real proud of, like me, for example. I don't think...."

"I'm sorry. You're right. It's just that he thinks she may know more than she's saying. That spidey-sense thing a lot of good interviewers have."

"Well, take it easy on her if you can. She's a special friend."

"Right. Got it. But we'll do what we have to do. You know that." There was a brief moment of silence, then Marsh changed the subject. "The other thing I called to tell you is that we're about ready to do a news conference and release of information to see if we can get some input to help us ID the remains. I don't think a lot more has come up since we talked about the lab's findings, but we've got something unique on three of the four of them. Victim A, the younger one, has a possible Georgia Southern connection and was apparently murdered by being shot in the chest. We don't have much on Victim B other than an estimate of his age. Victim C had the fancy belt buckle and alligator boots, and D is the older guy with the engraved wedding band. I'll give you pretty good odds that we're going to get some usable hits on the hotline. If we get a break in one of the four cases, a motive or even a suspect, the others will fall into line. Anyway, I'll keep you in the loop. Confidentially, of course. Keep listening out for the announcement. We'll probably go public this Friday. They tell me that's a good day—folks talk about it over the weekend. And we'll have things on the web—all the usual stuff."

I thanked Pete and hung up. One part of me felt I was betraying the woman I loved by not telling her what I knew, not warning her of the storm that was about to come. Another part of me, perhaps the rational one, said the investigators are faced with four horrific murders, all of which happened years ago. Somewhere out there somebody, the killer or killers, are thinking they got away with murder. No matter what happened next, someone was going to be very distraught.

It was Wednesday, two days later, before Jeanna called. "I'm sorry," she said. "I guess I keep saying that over and over.

Maybe I should have it tattooed on my forehead, or flashing in neon lights on my front door. I love you, John. You've got to know that, please. I appreciate everything you do and have done for me. I don't know what my life would be like without you. So, I'm begging you, please hang in there until we get past this. I don't want to lose you." I told her I loved her as well and was here if she needed me any time. I felt better, but words could not solve the problem.

On Friday, shortly after noon, Nate Dawson called on my cell. He was livid. "What the hell is going on here, John? I'm at work and some yahoo just came and said they found the skeletons of four bodies in a pond in northern Evans County. Wanted to know if that was my pond, 'cause he'd heard rumors."

"Who said that? I haven't heard anything."

"It was the police, the GBI people. It's on television, 'News at Noon' the guy said. It's that bastard Hodges, I just know it. So damned nice and polite and he was just waiting to put the knife in my back—in the backs of my wife and daughter, too. If he were here now I'd beat his sorry ass to a pulp."

"I'm sorry," I said, using that worn phrase for the nth time. "Let me make some phone calls and I'll get back to you as soon as I find out what's going on."

I decided to call Pete Marsh first. "You've got some awful mad people over in Claxton," I said.

"Yeah, I suspect you're talking about the Dawsons. They have every right to be, but they should be angry at whoever dumped the bodies, not at us. We're obligated to do what we're doing. I guess you could remind 'em they're victims, too, in a sense."

"Don't think that's gonna do a lot of good or make them feel much better." I thanked him, hung up and pulled out my phone to check the news feeds. The headlines, at least on the small screen, were boldly frightening: "Mass Murder? Remains of 4 Bodies Found in Rural Lake." "Investigators Seek Help in Solving 4 Evans County Murders." "Dumping Grounds for Murder Victims." "Is a Serial Killer on the Loose in South Georgia?" All were accompanied by reprints of a far less sensational press release from the GBI requesting the public's help regarding the four presumed homicides. A toll-free hotline number was given, and for the first time a reward was mentioned for information leading to "the arrest and conviction of the person or persons responsible for these crimes." All the articles said a news conference was scheduled for 4:00 p.m. at the Georgia Bureau of Investigation Regional Office in Statesboro. It would seem that things couldn't get much worse for the Dawsons.

CHAPTER 17

At 3:55 p.m., I was settled in an armchair in front of my office TV, staring blankly at commercials on the local CNN cable feed, waiting on the start of the 4:00 p.m. news conference. The revelation of the discovery of the remains of four unnamed, and presumably long-missing, individuals had turned an otherwise dull news day into a feeding frenzy for true-crime aficionados, all the more stoked by televised images of grave-voiced men and women sitting behind news desks awaiting the start of the event. In normal times, few would have heard of the small town of Claxton, Georgia, but now these same commentators sought to lend perspective by acquainting the waiting audience with the home of the "World Famous Claxton Fruit Cake," a staple of Christmas gifting and regifting for more than a century, or the little-known December 10, 1984 arrival of the Claxton Meteorite, "the only known meteor to directly strike a mailbox."

Promptly on the turn of the hour, the image switched to what appeared to be a conference room podium behind which stood Nelson Jackson, Pete Marsh's supervisor. I recognized Marsh and Randy Hodges who were with several other unfamiliar men standing in the background. After a brief welcome and introduction, Jackson began, "We're here today to ask for the public's help in solving what appear to be four murders committed over the last twelve to fifteen years. This is an unusual case, unlike anything we have investigated during my twenty-five years with the Bureau. Based on what we now know, each of the victims was male, was murdered and had their body hidden by being weighted down and thrown into a small pond in rural Evans County, a few miles north of

Claxton, Georgia. We believe the victims were killed at different times, estimated to range over a seven-to-eight year period, with the most recent body placed there five or six years ago. I do want to stress, however, that these dates are estimates and could be off either way by several years. No standard identifications such as drivers' licenses or the like were found, but each of the four had some unique characteristics that might lead to an identification. A moment ago I introduced Pete Marsh, who is the chief investigator on this case, and Randy Hodges, who is his second-in-command. Agent Marsh will speak to you first."

Over the next ten minutes, Marsh and subsequently Hodges gave a broad outline of the case, starting with the "accidental discovery of human bones by a fisherman," the use of a forensic dive team who discovered more, and finally the work done by the state crime laboratory. Their descriptions were vague, not revealing the Dawsons' names or the location of the pond. Marsh, now back at the podium, said, "As you have heard, we want to share in a limited way some of the findings resulting from our investigation and the good work of the crime lab. We have prepared a slide presentation that we'll show you now, and will be providing copies of it to every law enforcement agency in the state." As he spoke, the camera panned and zoomed in on a projection screen set to one side of the room. The conference room view was replaced by the screen image of the Dawson pond taken from the perspective of the small pasture.

"This is the crime scene, or if not where the murders occurred, where the bodies of the victims were hidden in a part of the lake twelve or more feet deep. Each body was weighted down to keep it from rising to the surface. We removed the water from the pond and completed our investigation, initially leaving the remains where they were discovered before removing them to the crime laboratory. There were the skeletal remains of four persons whom we identify as Victims A through D. We believe by releasing certain information about each one, there may be people who are able to provide insight into their identities. Also, today, for the first time, we are pleased to show you artists' renderings of what they may have looked like during life. These are based on the actual anatomy of the skulls and facial bones, and assisted by computer-based artificial intelligence programs designed for this purpose. I will start with Victim A."

The pond view was replaced by an almost photo-realistic image of the head and torso of a young man, perhaps around twenty years old, wearing a blue Georgia Southern polo shirt. "This is an artist's computer-assisted rendering of the youngest of the victims, whom we believe to be between eighteen and twenty-five years of age. He appears to have died from a gunshot wound to the chest and is the only one of the four for whom we have a presumed cause of death. The reason we are showing you his face and upper body is that he was wearing a Georgia Southern University shirt like this, and a pair of blue and white Nike athletic shoes when his body was placed in the pond." A picture of a Nike shoe similar to the one snagged on Robert's line filled the screen. "We have obtained a DNA profile of him, but no matches in any available databases have been found as yet. We suspect, but have no evidence for, the possibility that he was a college student or recent alumnus of Georgia Southern at the time of his death." An indistinct off-camera murmur could be heard, to which Marsh responded, "Just hold on, please. We'll be taking a few questions at the end of this presentation."

A new image appeared on the screen. "This is an image of

whom we refer to as Victim B. He is the person we know the least about. We believe he was between thirty and forty years of age. We have been unable thus far to extract a usable DNA profile, but I was told just yesterday the crime lab is still working on it. He was wearing a wedding ring, so we assume he was married." The artist's portrait was that of a younger white male with brown hair, large nose and prominent cheekbones. I was amazed how lifelike it appeared.

"For Victim C, we did discover what may be some important clues." A new image appeared on the screen, a younger white male, again with brown hair and an average appearing face. "Like Victim B, he appears to be between thirty and forty years old," Marsh continued. "The crime lab has tried, but do not believe they will be able to get a good DNA sample. However, he was found to be wearing a wide belt with a prominent handmade sterling silver buckle, which you can see here." A large image of the buckle now flashed on the screen. "We believe this to be typical of Navaho silverwork and may have belonged to someone who lived in or visited Arizona or New Mexico." He paused as new images appeared on screen showing an overview with closeup insets of a pair of high-topped western boots prominently displaying the distinctive pattern of alligator hide. "This person was also wearing what I am told would be a very expensive set of handmade alligator boots which, because of the material and its preservation, survived intact underwater for years. Importantly, the crime lab estimates that the body of this victim and the body of Victim B whom we presented a few moments ago, were possibly deposited in the pond at the same time, perhaps six or seven years ago, but again, the timing of their deaths is a rough guess.

"Finally, we have Victim D, and one very important clue discovered with his remains. This person was the oldest of the four, estimated to be in his fifties or early sixties. Here is the artist's impression of what he may have looked like when alive." The screen now displayed the face of a thin man whose dark hair was heavily sprinkled with gray. "Importantly, he was wearing a gold wedding band with the inscription 'H.W. & E.T.—6/1/1987' engraved on the inside. We believe this will be extremely important in determining his identity, but we have not as yet been able to do so. We hope providing these details to the public will yield some helpful clues and answers." The screen went dark as the camera panned back to the podium.

"We're prepared to take a few questions now, but please recall this is an ongoing investigation and there are limits on what we are willing to divulge at this point." Marsh said. "Before we move on to that, however, there is one very important announcement that we want to make. Due to the generosity of the governor of this state, a fund has been established to grant a reward of up to $10,000 for information leading to the arrest and conviction of a person or persons responsible for these crimes."

A number of hands apparently went up in the off-camera audience. "One at a time, please," Marsh said, pointing in the direction of the crowd. "Let's start with Mr. Parker there from the Savannah press." The camera rotated to focus on a middle-aged man gripping a spiral bound notebook.

"Mr. Marsh, can you tell us if the owner of this property is in any way a suspect in these crimes? You say the bodies were dumped there over a period of years. That would imply that whoever did that—and I'm presuming that was the murderer—would not return to the same site over and over unless he—or she—were certain their crimes would be unlikely to be discovered in that location. Doesn't that raise suspicion about the owner?"

I saw a look of dismay on Marsh's face, and could only imagine the reaction of Nate and Martha Dawson, and Jenna if they were watching. I grabbed the remote and switched off the television. What I had seen and heard was enough for one day.

CHAPTER 18

In the dog-eat-dog world of commercial media, the mysterious news of the four unidentified bodies became the top story of the day for the weekend editions of broadcast networks, print media and online news feeds alike. As was so often the case, the coverage of the presumed murders focused more on the bizarre nature of the alleged crimes, and speculation as to what sort of depraved criminal might claim responsibility for such acts. The victims, with their untimely ends and watery graves, appeared relegated to roles as supporting characters in the bigger story of why, how and who. As for the Dawsons, it seemed as if the real and potential harm to their lives and reputations was merely collateral damage, an unfortunate but not unexpected part of the larger picture. After all, were there not good reasons to consider them suspects as well?

All this worried me. As random as my discovery of the bone-filled shoe might have been, I could not help but somehow feel an unearned sense of responsibility. Karma seemed to have singled me out as the winner of the revenge-of-the-week competition. Late Saturday afternoon I tried calling the Dawsons on their cell and home phones. No answer. I did not leave a message. After debating whether I should or should not, I called Jenna's cell. Again, no answer, making it clear they were avoiding me. I wanted to be despondent, but instead I felt merely numb. I discovered long ago that there comes a point when one cannot absorb any more sorrow or negativity. When that mark is reached and exceeded, life continues on autopilot, free of happiness or sadness, but instead focused on survival. I was there.

I was not sure what to do, having apparently lost

involvement in the situation. I seriously doubted if the Dawsons would want me as their informal advisor and strongly suspected, as I had all along, that the fiasco of my fishing trip with Jenna's son meant a permanent end to our relationship. There was little that I could do. But, that did not mean I had lost interest in the presumed murders, or in knowing who killed the victims, and why. I silently decided to devote more time to the gallery, checking in every now and then with Pete Marsh in hopes that he would discreetly bring me up to date on the progress of the investigation. In the meantime, I would keep an open eye and ear on the media for any pertinent items of interest. For the remainder of the weekend and continuing into the following week, the stories available to the reading, watching or listening public were basically rehashes of the news conference the preceding Friday afternoon. There were several "on scene" reports filmed in front of the Evans County Courthouse in Claxton, most of which included interviews with Sheriff Hearn. These appeared to be mainly for show, as the sheriff's interview added nothing to what was already known. He specifically refused to identify the exact location of the "murder lake," as the Dawson pond had come to be known, or the identity of the owners of the property. Not having heard from Jenna or her parents, I had no idea what was actually happening.

On the following Friday, a week after the news conference, Pete Marsh called. "Hey," he said. "The Dawsons say you're off the case. We contacted Nate earlier today about some additional interviews, but when your name was mentioned, he bowed up and said you would not be there. I asked why, and it seems they want to blame you for all the publicity and controversy that this case is generating. I didn't talk with his wife." I didn't immediately respond, not sure what to say. Pete continued, "How about your girlfriend, Jenna?"

"I think I've been blacklisted by the whole family. I haven't spoken with any of them in a week, since before the news conference."

"Oh…." I got the impression Pete did not know exactly how to respond.

"Can you bring me up to date?" I asked.

Glad to move on to another, less sensitive topic, he readily agreed. "Sure! Not a lot of this is confidential, but treat it as such if you would."

"Okay."

"Just about the only thing to report is that our hotline has been far busier than we anticipated. We were expecting calls, of course, but we've almost been overwhelmed. Had to put on three operators to take the messages, and even then there are often times when we've got half a dozen folks on hold waiting to connect. In general, most of what we get on these tip lines is garbage, people speculating, offering their own theories and so on. The useful ones have been from people that know of, or have heard of someone who disappeared. Now, that doesn't mean they are dead, but rather they have lost contact with them. Lots of times it's family members who've become estranged. Sometimes it's a girl who's been dumped by a boyfriend, and just can't believe he's moved on with someone else. But…, we heard from a lady in Atlanta whose son was a student at Georgia Southern. He was a junior, about twenty or twenty-one years old. He supposedly disappeared while on spring break in Florida. The story was that he drowned in the ocean at Daytona Beach or one of those beachfront towns in north Florida. They never found his body, and from what I've been told she said to the operator, the story of his going missing is kinda fishy—pardon the pun there. I don't have the details in front of me, but the time frame would fit for Victim A. It will probably turn out to be a dead end, but the guys at the office are following up." Marsh didn't apologize for his second pun this time.

"Do you have a name for him?"

"Yeah, it was Willingham, or something like that. Can't remember his first name."

"There's nothing on the belt buckle or wedding band guys?

"Nothing useful. But I've got to stress that just separating the wheat from the chaff in these hotline call-ins is a big job in itself. You don't want to miss anything, but you intuitively know a lot of what you get is well-meaning but useless, and a lot is just pure BS."

I thanked Pete and asked him to keep me updated if he wouldn't mind. "I'll be glad to, but remember, this is all off the record. One of the reasons I want to keep you current is because of where it looks like the investigation is heading. I don't know if you saw that news conference a week ago, but on the very first question that reporter, Parker from the Savannah Morning News, implied the owner of the pond where the bodies were found should be considered a suspect. Personally, I believe the Dawsons are among the victims here. I think there's a snowball's chance in hell that they had anything at all to do with the killings, and that also implies they did not know about them. But, again, you've got to turn over every stone, follow every lead, no matter how improbable or uncomfortable it may seem. You are the only person who seems to know the Dawsons, and up until last week, the only person they said they would trust. I think—no, I'm sure—once the dust settles y'all will kiss and make up and you'll be back in their good graces. Isn't that what you want? Or do you want to give up on your friend, Jenna?"

"You know it's what I want, Pete, but I'm not going to rat out the woman I love, or for that matter, her parents."

"Okay, let me ask you this question. What if you found out that they did in fact have something to do with the murders, or that they knew the bodies were there and were covering for whoever dumped them? Would you still want to join that family by marrying the daughter?"

Pete was correct. By his reasoning, I had nothing to lose. I would just be doing what the lawyers I used to work with referred to as "due diligence." Looking at it from that aspect, it almost seemed reasonable. What if Jenna and I were together as before? Would I be morally, ethically or legally required to report her or her parents if they knew? The only acceptable answer had to be "yes." Could I live with myself after such a betrayal of trust? On the other hand, if Jenna and I were to carry our relationship to marriage, the ultimate level of trust, what would I do then? All these thoughts rushed through my mind at what seemed like light speed. I said, "I love Jenna. I trust her. I'll stick by her no matter what."

CHAPTER 19

"So, you want to continue as is?" Pete asked. "Look, John, I want to keep you acquainted with what happens. I know you pretty well. I trust you, and I hope you feel that you can trust me. You know the situation as well or better than anyone else, and importantly, you know the players thus far—in a way, you're one of them. I respect your intelligence and your insight. I don't want to lose touch. I think you can help make some valuable contributions to this investigation, even if we sort of keep things off the official record."

Despite my confusion and mixed feelings, I said, "Sounds reasonable to me. But we'll take it a day at a time. Tell me more, though, about the woman who said her son disappeared in Florida on spring break. Have you followed up on that?"

"Not yet, and I'm not sure when we'll get to it. Four unsolved murders is a huge case, but you've got to keep in mind that this is not something that just happened. All these men were killed years ago. The old line about murders that are not solved in the first forty-eight hours is kind of true, but we're obviously way beyond that. I'd prefer that we take our time, carefully consider what we know and what we don't, and then chase after the clues and evidence most likely to yield results. If the kid allegedly disappeared in Florida, we'll interview the woman to be sure, but I wouldn't put much stock in the outcome. To give you an example of the sort of crap we get on the hotline, a couple of days ago we had a call from a retired undertaker from some small town over in west Georgia, a guy named Elmo Kantt. He said he was sure the four dead men were victims of an unscrupulous funeral director who had been paid to have the bodies of the deceased cremated. But to save money, the guy dumps them in the pond and then gives the families urns filled with ashes from his fireplace. Possible, yeah, but likely, no way. There will be a lot like that, I can promise you."

Even though Pete promised to keep me up to date, for practical purposes my involvement in the case, and more importantly with Jenna and the Dawsons, seemed to be over. I tried devoting myself to the gallery, much to the annoyance of Jessica, who with my recent frequent absences had gotten used to running things herself. Sales and business in general remained good. She reminded me that she would be sure to call if I had to be away and something came up. I thought about taking a few days off, maybe going on some sort of vacation, but I rapidly realized that there was no place I wanted to go. The truth was, I missed Jenna. Time would heal the wounds, I told myself.

Two more weeks dragged past. I decided to educate myself on something new to keep me distracted, but could not muster the interest in much of anything. Late on a Thursday afternoon I was in my apartment watching reruns of movies on cable when my cell phone buzzed. I looked at the screen and saw Jenna's number. Taking a deep breath and trying to sound calm, I pressed the green "Accept" icon on the screen. After a moment of silence, a small voice said, "Mr. John?"

"Yes, who is this?"

"It's Robert, your friend. You took me fishing, remember?" How could I forget…?

"Hey, it's good to hear from you. Why are you calling me? Does your mother know?"

"No, she's taking a nap right now. I'm calling on her phone."

"Okay, well…, it's good to talk with you."

"I'm calling because my mama misses you. She's been real upset ever since you had a fight or something or whatever happened. She wouldn't tell me. But now she stays sad all the time and doesn't want to do anything, and sometimes late at night I can hear her crying. She won't tell me what's wrong, but I figured it out. All this started when you had a fight. I heard my granddaddy and her talking and he said she had to stay away from you, and...."

"Whoa, Robert. Do you think you should be calling me without her permission?"

"Mr. John, I am almost ten years old, and my granddaddy talks about me being 'the man of the house now,' and my mama is sad and pouting all the time and I know it's because she misses you. Somebody has got to do something and I guess that's my job now. I want to know if you will call her so you can get back together and things will be good like they were before."

There was a rustling noise and I heard Jenna's voice in the background. "Robert, who are you talking to? Is that my phone? Where did you get that?"

Another rustling noise, then Jenna's voice again, "Hello. Who is this?"

"It's me, John."

"What are you doing calling here? You're...."

"I didn't call. Robert called me."

Silence, then, "Oh, he did?"

"Yes, he said you were sad, and that you've been upset."

A shorter pause this time, then, "Things have been difficult, yes."

"Do you want to talk?" I asked.

"Let me think about it. Don't call me. I'll call you. And in the future I'll make sure Robert doesn't have access to my phone."

"Okay." I didn't know what else to say.

"Well, uh…, goodbye then, I guess."

"Yeah, goodbye."

I waited for her to end the call, hoping that she would find something else to say. We both remained on the line. After what seemed like an eternity, Jenna said, "I miss you terribly, John." The line then went dead.

For the first time in what seemed like several weeks, I slept well that night. Shortly after eight the following morning Pete Marsh called. It was the first I had heard from him in a couple of weeks. "Looks like we've got a break, John, something real this time and worth investigating. You remember Victim D, the older guy with the engraved wedding band? A couple of weeks ago the hotline got a call from a woman in Savannah, said she had been 'seeing' a widowed man named Howard Wilson. His wife had died a little less than a year earlier, and he was just beginning to get out and go on a few dates. She didn't know his exact age, but he was around sixty, and she recalls that he said he was quite a few years off from retirement. The thing was, he insisted on wearing the wedding band from his marriage, something about a promise he made to his wife on her deathbed. Said he'd take it off if or when he got married again. You probably don't remember but the initials on the ring were 'H.W. & E.T.' and the date '6/1/1987'. It sounded like a hot tip, so we got right on it and sent a couple of guys out to interview the woman. At the time she was dating this Wilson guy, she'd just gotten divorced, and sort of implied that both of them were 'dating around,' seeing several people. Well, to make a long story short, it seemed to her that they were getting kinda serious, and then he just stopped calling. She called him several times, but he wouldn't answer, so she gave up and moved on. She couldn't give us an exact date, but it seems to be around the time the crime lab thinks his body was dumped in the pond.

"Now, here's the interesting part, we tracked down who Howard Wilson was, and found that he had been married to a woman named Elizabeth Tinley, with the marriage certificate dated June 1, 1987, the same date on the ring. And a woman named Elizabeth T. Wilson was confirmed to have died of breast cancer about ten months or so before the caller said she had first started seeing him. We searched all the usual databases in the southeastern U.S., but there is no evidence of a recorded death certificate in the name of Howard Wilson in the time frame we're looking at. Apparently, the Wilsons never had any children, so you might think it's possible that there was not much follow-up if he simply disappeared. We don't have a lot more than that right now. We're working on finding out where he lived, where he worked and that sort of thing. If we can find any family members or interview his employer it'll let us know if we need to keep searching or move on to something else."

CHAPTER 20

The possible connection to the older victim appeared important. But while the GBI investigators were digging into the curious and compelling circumstances described by his former girlfriend, there was no evidence that the man named Howard Wilson was in fact dead. In a world where it is nearly impossible to exist without leaving a digital or paper trail of some sort, the most important "evidence" would be its absence. The use of a cell phone, cash withdrawn from an ATM, a tank of gas paid for by credit card, anything of that nature that could be found might indicate this was nothing more than another false path, a rabbit hole of sorts in this already bizarre situation. I said to Pete, "Sounds fascinating. Please let me know if or when you decide he may be one of the bodies. And while we're talking, have your guys had a chance to follow up with the woman who thought the remains of the youngest victim might be those of her son?"

"Not yet. We haven't written that off, but as I said before, it's lower down on our list. We're looking first at what appear to be the most promising leads. Honestly, if what she says is correct about him being drowned in Florida, I don't really see how he could have ended up in a small lake more than 250 miles away in south Georgia.

"We did get a hot lead just yesterday afternoon, though, on Victim C, the guy with the silver belt buckle and alligator boots. Some woman from Texas called thinking it might be her ex-husband, a fellow named Miguel Juarez. She said he had a buckle that looked similar but wasn't sure it was the same, that he often wore a pair of alligator boots, and went missing about the right time to match when the body was dumped.

The story—her story, anyway—is that he was a salesman for a heavy equipment company. His territory covered Georgia, Florida and Alabama, and he would stay on the road about ten days a month, traveling around to dealerships in those states and doing whatever it is that salesmen do. He'd call home most days, but sometimes he wouldn't, especially when he was taking customers out to dinner, that kind of thing. She was used to that. At the time, he was staying in a motel in Brunswick and working an area as far south as Jacksonville and as far north as Savannah. Well, when she hadn't heard from him in more than forty-eight hours, she called his cell. Went straight to voicemail. After twenty-four hours more of that, she called his boss, who hadn't heard from him either. I'll spare you the details, but the boss flew in to Jacksonville, then went up to the motel in Brunswick where the guy was supposed to be staying. His stuff was still in the room, but his car was missing. No sign of violence, or anything like that. So, the cops get called in, and pretty soon find his car in long-term parking at the Savannah airport, but no evidence he got on a flight out, in fact the videos never showed that he entered the terminal.

"The wife said they were having marital problems, probably because he was on the road a lot of the time and she suspected he was seeing other women. The local law enforcement did some investigating, but never found anything. The wife filed for divorce based on 'abandonment,' and has moved on, in fact, she's remarried. So we're going after that one as soon as we can. A couple of my guys are flying out to Texas next week."

All this, my interest and personal, though peripheral, involvement in the case was something I could not have prevented or avoided. I appreciated Pete Marsh wanting to keep me informed, but it increasingly looked like I should formally get out, once and for all. I believed Jenna when she said, "I miss you terribly," but that could be like saying how much she missed the sun's warmth in the dead of winter. Nothing was likely to change. If I accepted reality, I had to realize that it was mainly curiosity that maintained my connection to the murder cases. I decided I needed to get away, take a few days off for a "business trip," or somesuch tax-deductible journey far away from Savannah. Out of my familiar environment, away from the clues and prompts that made me think of Jenna and my future with her, maybe I would find the courage to make some hard decisions. After perusing several art magazines, I chose Scottsdale, Arizona, one of the undisputed meccas of western art—cowboys, horses, buffalo—schlocky stuff, but it sells. With a few quick phone calls, I had booked roundtrip airfare from Savannah to Phoenix and a hotel room in central Scottsdale within walking distance of Main Street with its museums and more than two dozen galleries. I would be leaving the next afternoon.

I called Jessica and told her I would be going out of town for a few days on sort of a buying trip. She said she did not anticipate any problems but would call if anything came up. She couldn't resist asking, "I guess this last-minute trip means you and Jenna have kissed and made up?"

"Probably just the opposite, Jessica. I need to make some hard decisions about the relationship, and want to get away from the distractions here so I can do some thinking. And I'm sure I'll be looking at what's new and what's selling. Probably buy a few things for the gallery."

"Have fun, then." From the tone of her voice I doubted if she believed me.

The flight to Phoenix—via Atlanta, of course—was uneventful. I ubered from the airport to the hotel, checked in and took a long nap. For the next three days, I went from gallery to gallery, looking at art, discussing business trends with the owners, and visiting the various museums in Phoenix and Scottsdale. In the evenings, after a good dinner and a couple of glasses of wine, I tried to decide once and for all what to do about my situation. On the morning of the fourth day, now relaxed and with my mind made up to end things with Jenna, I packed, checked out and stood outside the hotel for a moment marveling at the clear blue Arizona sky. "Things are going to be okay," I told myself. "It's been rough, it's going to be rough, but you've been through worse." Though years had passed, I thought about the pain of the breakup of my first marriage, and with it, the loss of contact with my two children. I wished so much that I could wipe that memory from my mind and start anew. It wasn't going to happen. I was no fool. Some scars cannot be seen, but that doesn't mean they are not just as real. At that moment my thoughts were interrupted as my taxi for the airport pulled up.

After enduring the lines and the hassle of airport security, I grabbed a sandwich at a concourse food kiosk and settled in at the gate, waiting for boarding to begin. Just at that moment my cell phone vibrated and beeped, indicating I had received a text. I did not recognize the number, but the message was both clear and chilling. "YOU BETTER BACK OFF. I KNOW WHO YOU ARE, WHAT YOU DO AND WHERE YOU LIVE. IF YOU DON'T YOU'RE GOING TO END UP LIKE THE OTHERS, BUT THIS TIME NO ONE IS GOING TO BE ABLE TO FIND YOUR BODY."

A sense of shock and fear seemed to pour over me as I sat, waiting. An elderly woman seated facing me just across the aisle said, "Are you all right, son? You look like you just saw a ghost."

"I'm fine," I said, trying to sound that way. "Just an

unexpected message." The woman nodded and resumed reading her book.

I reread the message and looked at the number again. The area code was 912. Assuming the sender lived in that area—and that was by no means certain—the phone was registered somewhere in southeast coastal Georgia: Savannah, Brunswick, Vidalia, Waycross, or…, Claxton. I reasoned this had to be a message sent to the wrong number. It seemed to refer to the murders, but it could be about almost anything, a joke even. And on top of that, I wasn't really involved in the case. Pete Marsh or Randy Hodges or anyone else I had met from the GBI wouldn't have said anything. Probably some guy in a dispute with some other guy, threatening him. But what did the reference to "the others" mean? And was the sender serious about "this time no one is going to be able to find your body?"

This had to be a mistake, or a joke or…. At that point the gate agent called my boarding group. I stuffed the phone back in my pocket and vowed to call Pete Marsh as soon as I got back to Savannah.

CHAPTER 21

"Damn, John, that would scare the holy crap out of me," Pete Marsh said. I was sitting on Concourse D of the Atlanta airport awaiting my flight to Savannah. I had called him as soon as I had gotten off the plane.

"Yeah, but what do I do? Is someone out to get me?"

"Read the text to me again," Pete said. I did. He said, "Gimme a minute to think." After a moment he began, "Okay, let's both try to relax and think about this rationally. This is speculating, of course, but I think it's one of three things. First, and in a worst-case scenario, somebody knows you're tangentially connected with the case and is trying to scare you off. Second, it's a joke, and a really sick, bad, inappropriate one at that. Or third, it's a mistake. Someone sent it to your phone but intended it for someone else. And if you want to hear my assessment, the likelihood of those is in the reverse order: a mistaken phone number first, a bad joke second, and as a distant third, someone wanting you out of the picture in having anything to do with the murder investigation. Think about it, John. Who knows you have anything at all to do with this case? You don't really, just me keeping you up to speed about some of what's happening. I don't mention ninety-nine percent of what goes on because it's boring or not important or just plain routine."

"Sure, but what do I do? Where do we go? Should you get officially involved?"

"Like I said earlier," Pete replied, "there are lots of possibilities, but there are just so many you can be prepared for. I read somewhere not long ago that thousands of meteors make it through the atmosphere and hit earth each year, but over the last hundred years there is only one known instance of a person being struck by one. It happened in 1954, some woman in Sylacauga, Alabama. It would be devastating if you got hit, but the probability of that happening is infinitesimally small. That's how I see this text you received. If it was a mistake, maybe sent to the wrong number, you shouldn't worry about it. That's the most likely thing. If it were a bad joke, the same thing, just remember to slug the person who sent it next time you see him—or her. And on the extremely remote chance somebody knows you're connected, why would they want you off the case? Why would they threaten you with bodily harm? So you gotta ask, who knows?" He waited for my reply.

"The only people who really know are members of law enforcement, and the Dawsons, including Jenna, I guess."

"You think someone from our team sent it? C'mon, John...."

"So you think maybe Nate or Martha, or..., Jenna?"

"No, of course not. Be reasonable. Jenna is not going to send that kind of shit, or Martha Dawson, either. You should know that. Now, Nate, it's possible but not probable. He's mad at you for sure, but deep down he knows you care about his daughter. And I should say 'unmarried daughter with a kid and a history on her.' Kind of a turn-off for most guys looking for long-term relationships." Pete's words burned, but he was correct.

"So, what should I do? Where do we go?" I asked again.

"I'd recommend you just sit down and enjoy the sunshine. Watch your back, of course. Be on the lookout for anything suspicious or out of the ordinary, but otherwise live your life as you would anyway. As for us, the GBI, the text is a threat of sorts, so I can justify using some resources to follow up on it. I'll have our guys run the phone number and see what we come up with. It's possible we can get a name or even a location. Depends on a lot of factors. Do you think you can live with that?"

My gut reaction was to reply with a snarky "Do I have a choice?" but instead said, "I'll do my best. Thank you for helping out." I read him the phone number associated with the text. He said he would be in touch when he had something to report. I looked at my watch. My flight to Savannah was still two hours away. I went to the bar and ordered a double bourbon to settle my nerves.

At work the following morning, all appeared calm and relaxed. Jessica had closed a couple of large sales during my absence. I praised her work and gave her a spontaneous hundred-dollar bonus. Hattie, my bookkeeper, checked in. All seemed well financially. I looked up the tracking data for several artworks I had purchased in Arizona and was having shipped to Savannah. I kept wanting to pick up my phone and call Jenna, but resisted the urge. I would have as much success pleading with her as I would trying to resurrect the dead.

A week after my return, Pete Marsh called. I had been expecting to hear from him any day about the investigation into the text. It seems that everything is digital these days; it shouldn't be that difficult. "Hey, John, got some very interesting news for you, and this is extremely confidential. Remember I told you about the Wilson guy who was dating the woman from Savannah, then just sort of broke it off suddenly? I sent a couple of guys to interview her, and we started digging into various public records and so on. We have what I think will be a good ID now, the first of the four victims. So, sit down and listen to what's cropped up.

"First, the guy's name was Howard Maurice Wilson. Assuming we have estimated correctly when his body was dumped in the pond, he would have been about fifty-nine or sixty years old. And if you remember, he was married to a lady named Elizabeth Tinley, who died of breast cancer less than a year before that. We're guessing here at the dates, of course. They had no children and he had no known living relatives. The Tinley family didn't like Wilson, said Elizabeth married down, but everyone agreed they were happy and that he was devastated by her death, as you might expect.

"So, as a married couple they were living in Reidsville, where Mrs. Wilson worked in a convenience store and Howard commuted to work in Claxton every day. It's only about fifteen miles. When the wife became terminally ill, he took a leave of absence from his work to care for her, but after her death, he came back full time...."

"Where did he work?" I interrupted.

"Just hold on, I'll get to that. Anyway, being newly widowed and living in a small town in kinda the middle of nowhere, after his wife's death Howard sells their house and rents an apartment on the west side of Savannah. He told his friends that since his wife's passing he needed a change, to live somewhere he could meet new friends and presumably have a better social life—that last part is my conclusion, anyway. So he moves to Savannah, starts dating around, and seemed to be getting over his wife's death. He developed a new set of friends and went out a lot, it seems from what we could learn. He still commuted to work every day, but this time his drive was about forty-five or fifty minutes each way, most of it on the interstate. Not too bad.

"Now, here's the kicker. Wilson worked at a wood chip mill, McKinsey Forest Products, where he was a shift supervisor. It was a job he'd had a long time, and one of the best paying there in the plant. They said when we interviewed them that he just didn't show up for work one day. All this happened a number of years ago, of course, but even then the people in management who'd been there back then said he was a great guy, straight as an arrow, and one of the best workers they had. Well, when he quit showing up and no one could get ahold of him, they gave a temporary promotion to the employee who had worked in that position when Howard took the leave of absence to attend to his wife. He was also described as a good employee, too, and in fact is still employed there as a shift supervisor."

"Pete, you're not saying what I think you…," I began.

"Yes, I am. That guy, the replacement for Howard Wilson, was none other than Nate Dawson, who still has the job now years later."

"My god," I said. "That sort of changes the picture doesn't it?"

"It can, but it just doesn't feel right. Sure, Nate moves to the top of the suspect list, but for some reason I just can't see him as a mass murderer. The place where the bodies were thrown and how they were weighted down would seem to suggest that a single individual was responsible, but I don't want to jump the gun here. No one's going anywhere and there's no statute of limitations on the crime of murder. So, we're going to proceed slowly, carefully and meticulously before we make any moves at all toward an arrest."

"Do you think Nate is the one who sent me the text message?" I asked.

"I seriously doubt it. Maybe not as much as before, but I still can't fit that piece in the puzzle."

CHAPTER 22

"What about tracking down the phone that sent the text?" I asked Pete.

"Oh, sorry, I almost forgot. We were able to determine that the number was assigned to a cheap prepaid cell phone purchased from Cricket Wireless at one of their Savannah stores. The name and address listed for the buyer turned out to be bogus. And as far as could be figured out, the phone has not been used to make calls, and only to send texts a handful of times. There's nothing we could retrieve about the contents of the texts or who they were sent to. Since no conventional calls were logged from that phone, it didn't ping any towers, meaning there's no usable location information. I know that all sounds strange—at least it did to me—but I'm told that when someone wants to block his location or other personal information with a cell phone, that's how it's done. The modern version of the unsigned poison pen letter."

"So, no luck there...."

"I'm afraid not, and don't ask me again what you should do. Wake up, John, you're a big boy, a grown man who has been through a lot worse than what's going on now. Yes, I know how you feel about Jenna, but you're not responsible for any of this, and in spite of that you've stuck in there with the Dawsons and done everything you can to be helpful. Relax, take a few days off, go...."

"I just got back from a vacation, remember?"

"Oh, well, and I'll say this for the last time, things will work out. Chill! It's all gonna be okay."

Sometimes when you're confused and don't know what to do, the best thing is to listen to someone who sees the bigger picture, and take their advice to heart. I resolved to do just that. Then Jenna called.

"Hey," she said, meekly. "I had to call you…, I…, uh…."

"Are you okay?"

"Yeah, just angry with myself for my stupidity. I was listening to my dad, and his yapping about how you started all this, and how could I tolerate being around someone who would not support me when times got rough, stuff like that. I didn't feel it, and I didn't want to believe it, but he countered that by accusing me of being desperate and 'blinded by what I thought was love'—those were his exact words—and so I believed him and reacted and tried to cut you off, to push you out of my mind. Thinking back on it, it looks like Robert was the only one who saw through that, saw the real me. Will you forgive me, and let me try to make it up to you somehow?"

"You know the answer to that, Jenna. You know I will. But I've got to be truthful, the investigation about the bodies is moving ahead, and I'm not sure where it will lead."

"What does that have to do with us? You and me?"

"Nothing I hope. I'm just saying there's been a lot of publicity, a lot of unfounded rumors, attempts to drag you or your parents into this just because you own the pond. I know there's light at the end of the tunnel, but we're not there yet."

Jenna said nothing for a few seconds, then, "Are you saying that maybe somehow my parents or me are involved?"

"No, of course not, but I was told the investigators still want more interviews to get a better idea of who might have had access, who knew the gate lock combination, or how to find the key to the boat lock to…."

"So you still think it might be one of us?" Jenna's voice had suddenly turned cold.

"No, not at all. I'm just trying to say that the investigation is not over yet, and…."

"That's fine," Jenna blurted out. "I shouldn't have called. Forget what I said." The line went dead.

Sometimes I think I am my own worst enemy. If you had asked me the day before Jenna's call what I secretly wanted most, it would have been just that. I was the one who should feel stupid, not Jenna. I should have kept my mouth shut and said a silent prayer of thanks. Instead I now felt more like the fool who plunged into a stormy sea to save a drowning man, forgetting that he didn't know how to swim. I should have listened to Pete Marsh's advice to leave well enough alone. I resolved to push the Dawsons, including Jenna, the bodies, and the whole investigation to the back of my mind. Given the circumstances, there was no reason at all for my involvement other than my natural curiosity. I knew Pete would keep me informed, but that would be the limit of my contact with the whole matter.

That resolution lasted for two days, broken by another call from Pete Marsh. "Hey, John, to quote Alice, things just keep getting curiouser and curiouser. Remember Victim B, one of the two that we thought might have been placed in the pond around the same time. The other one was the silver belt buckle guy whose ex-wife contacted us. 'B' was in his thirties or forties and wearing a plain wedding band, suggesting he was married, but up until now that's about all we had. I think I mentioned the lab was working on extracting some DNA, and they finally got a profile. They're looking at some databases now, trying to find a connection with a family member. So that gives us two DNA profiles, but no connections as yet."

"Anything going on with the Dawsons? Or Jenna?" I immediately regretted asking.

"Not really. At some point we may have to figure out a

way to get them to testify under oath. I didn't believe it was going to come to this. I still think that line of inquiry leads nowhere, but like I said before, you gotta turn over every stone."

"Thanks, Pete. I really appreciate your call, but don't you think it's time I backed off completely? It looks like Jenna and I have split up for good, and there's no reason to keep me informed because the Dawsons obviously don't want me around. I can just wait and get my news like everyone else."

"Okay, if that's what you want...," Pete hesitated before continuing, "...but let me do this. I'll call you for one of two reasons: first, if we get a really big break in the case, and second, if we find out that the Dawsons—and that includes Jenna—are in any way connected to the victims or their murders. Will that work for you?"

"Why should it? Why do I need to know?"

"Because I know you too well. You have, or now 'had,' I guess, plans to marry Jenna. I know it will satisfy your curiosity and let you find out what you missed." Pete did in fact know me too well.

"All right," I said, knowing this was the end. With Jenna, the Dawsons, and the plans for our—now my—future. The final nail in the coffin.

Suddenly, it seemed, my world changed. It was like waking up one morning, walking into your kitchen for a cup of coffee and discovering that someone had completely rearranged everything overnight. The comforting familiarity had disappeared, forcing you to think about every move, find a new chair to sit in and a new table on which to prop your elbows. When Jenna or the immediate past poked into my thoughts, I consciously worked to change the subject, bury the memories and reflections. The first couple of weeks were the hardest. Pete kept his word and did not contact me. I did my best to become more involved in the day-to-day operation of the gallery, much to Jessica's annoyance no doubt. I even took a customer out to dinner, a thirtyish, newly divorced lady who seemed interested in getting to know me better. Despite my best efforts, I kept mentally comparing her with Jenna. Getting over my obsession with her was far more difficult and complicated than I ever could have imagined. After about a month, life seemed to improve. My bookkeeper Hattie, always willing to offer sage advice garnered over a lifetime, pronounced me depressed and strongly suggested I consider taking medicine "for just a while, to help you cope." I refused, at the same time realizing she was probably correct in her diagnosis.

It had been exactly five weeks after my last conversation with Pete Marsh before he called once again. I answered with, "Pete, I thought you said you would not be calling…."

"I believe I said I would call if one of two things came up, a big break in the case, or possible evidence of involvement by the Dawsons. Wanna hear the news or do you want me to wish you a good day and hang up?"

I swallowed hard, feeling like a recovering addict who just been offered "a little hit." "Tell me what you've got," I said, thinking this wouldn't set back my ongoing recovery.

CHAPTER 23

"Okay, here goes," Pete said. "A lot has happened since we last spoke. And John, you've been acting so damned peculiar about all this, I want to let you know that the minute you've heard enough, or maybe just don't want to hear any more, say so and I'll stop talking. You're still a great guy who I admire and respect, but for you this is a sensitive subject and you can be the boss. Got it?"

"Got it."

"To start, remember the two middle-aged guys, 'B' and 'C', the one with the plain wedding band and the silver buckle guy? We sort of suspicioned they were put in the pond at the same time, but hadn't found a possible connection until now. If you remember, the buckle guy, we called him Victim C, but found out his name was Miguel Juarez, worked as a heavy equipment salesman. He had just disappeared without a trace. His wife filed for divorce, which of course he didn't contest because he was dead, but no one knew that at the time. For the other guy, the lab had trouble finding a usable DNA sample at first, but eventually did and started looking for relatives across south Georgia. They finally got a hit for a female DNA match which led them to an elderly couple in a nursing home, the Kleins. The husband has Alzheimer's but the wife's pretty intact mentally. She'd gotten into genealogy and sent in a DNA test for herself. It turned out to be a partial genetic match for that of her son, Victim B, a married guy named Gary Klein who lived in Jacksonville, Florida. Or I should say did live in Jacksonville, but had disappeared some seven or eight years earlier, basically abandoning his wife and two kids. He said he was going out for the night with a business friend, didn't say where but did tell the wife he would be home late. About eleven o'clock that night, he called his wife to say they had been drinking, and the friend was too drunk to drive him home, so they were going to spend the night in a motel and he'd be back the next morning. If he told her where he was at the time, she didn't remember it. Of course he never came back. There was a big search that focused on the Brunswick and Jacksonville areas, and eventually he became another unsolved missing person case to add to the list. Klein was the business manager for a fairly large construction company, and as you might expect, bought or leased heavy equipment. So, it seems likely he would go out drinking with a salesman like Juarez picking up the tab. And it also appears we can reasonably infer they were killed at the same time and most likely by the same person. I think this is pretty solid, which means we have three out of four of the remains ID'ed."

"Interesting," I said, "but it doesn't sound like you have any clue about who killed them."

"True...."

"Or for that matter how and why they ended up in a pond in rural Evans County."

"I think that's pretty obvious, and we're going after that next. We have avoided doing more interviews with the Dawsons, mainly because of their hostility and what's likely to be their lack of cooperation. We were trying to get as much info—and ammunition—as possible before talking with them again. I believe we've reached that point."

"But you still don't have anything on Victim A, the younger guy with the Nike shoes and Georgia Southern shirt?" I asked.

"No, and that's one of the things that surprises me the most. We've got a lot on him, how he was dressed, his DNA and so on, and I really thought he'd be the first set of remains we'd attach a name to, but no...."

"What about the woman whose son supposedly drowned on spring break in Florida?"

"That is such a long shot...." Pete's voice trailed off. "I guess we'll get to working on it soon, but these other connections seem more on point."

"But you still don't have any clear evidence of the Dawsons' involvement in any of this, do you?" I asked. "For the Wilson fellow, the shift supervisor whose job Nate Dawson took over, I can see something there, but when you realize there are three other dead men with no obvious connection at all, the idea that Nate might have a role in all this seems pretty remote."

"I agree, but I keep harping on following up on every hint, not making too many assumptions about things or situations that may appear obvious at first blush. Or not so obvious. Any role that Nate might have played falls in that category."

"Sounds like you're making progress," I said.

"I think so, but we're nowhere near the end I'm afraid. That's about all I've got for an update," Pete said, then asked, "Do you have any questions, John?"

"Not really. Any word on Jenna? It's been hard breaking it off with her."

"I'm sure. And no, nothing there. I'm certain we'll want to interview her father again, but I have a feeling that unless something totally unexpected raises its ugly head, we won't need to talk with Jenna."

"Okay, then," Pete said, signaling he was ready to end the conversation. "Tell me one thing before I hang up. Are you still fine with my checking in to update you every once in a while?"

"Yeah, I guess," I said. "It is what it is. I have to learn to face reality."

I simply could not see Nate Dawson arranging for the murder of the Wilson man so he could take his blue-collar hourly job at the wood chip mill. It made no sense economically or otherwise. And couple that with the idea of Nate disposing of the body on his own property, that sounded beyond ridiculous. He had too much plain common sense for that. He was only making things worse for himself by his hostile attitude toward the investigation and the negative notoriety that unfortunately came with it. I hoped his repeat interview would go better than expected, that he would convince his inquisitors of his non-involvement.

The one unknown that bothered me most was Jenna. I did truly love her, but had become so focused on convincing her to marry me that I realized I was losing perspective. The recent long break in our relationship, the hours of ruminating about what we were as a couple and what we might be as man and wife, had possibly caused me to lose my objectivity. "Blinded by what I thought was love," to repeat Nate Dawson's words about Jenna's view of her relationship with me. But wasn't that the way things were supposed to be? Everyone has their flaws, and no relationship is completely perfect. We live in a world filled with the constant compromises necessary to make it through each day of our lives. The concept of love, at least as I understand it, is that we acknowledge each other's faults and imperfections, agreeing in advance that they are accepted and forgiven. The thing that frightened me the most was the unknown or possibly unknowable Jenna. The woman I loved was the one I knew, contrite, willing to admit her past errors and transgressions, and sworn to make life better for herself, for her son, and at one time, for me. Were there ugly things that I did not know about her? The answer would be "yes," of course.

And was I willing to forgive them in advance without knowing the exact nature or wickedness of those things? I had been willing to say "yes" to that as well, but now the question seemed moot.

I was aware of Jenna's past history of drug abuse; in fact we had first met in a court-mandated aftercare program. I knew she had worked in a "gentleman's club," actively engaged in the lifestyle that implied and required. I knew of the failure of her marriage, though never demanded she reveal the details, offer mea culpas or justifications. To me she had become an open book; she was what she appeared to be, a beautiful, intelligent woman with a sensitive and loving soul, someone who cared about me and forgave my faults and past sins as I had forgiven hers.

I knew the GBI investigators would want to question Jenna at least one more time. That bothered me. The prime concern was who had access to the Dawson pond. Yes, there were church picnics and the like, things Nate and Martha Dawson would have hosted. The variety of those attending would have been limited to their friends and fellow parishioners, not a worrisome group to be sure. But in terms of sheer numbers, it had to be inferred that most of the visitors to the pond were Jenna's friends and acquaintances from high school, college, her wedding, and her time in Savannah after the divorce from Carl. There could be other things as well; I did not know and had not wanted to ask. I was sure the GBI's interviewers would though, perhaps under oath at some point. That prospect frightened me.

CHAPTER 24

To my surprise, Pete Marsh called again two days later. "I hadn't expected to hear from you so soon," I said.

"And I hadn't expected to be calling. Just wanted to let you know we're shutting down most of the investigation on the 'Dawson Pond Cases,' as we're calling it around here."

"Why? You said you thought you might be cutting back, but not quitting. What happened?"

"The usual," Pete said. "What always happens with government bureaucracies, issues of funding and personnel. I got a call last night from Nelson Jackson, the guy I report to. After saying great things about the work we've been doing, he began throwing around words like 'personnel constraints,' and 'budgetary considerations,' and 'other more pressing obligations.' So I knew what was coming. Basically he told me to wrap up the investigation. He wants me to continue as the nominal lead investigator, assisted by Randy Hodges, but it will be very much part time for us. We'll focus on it only if something new comes up. We've got thirty days, then it's on to other things."

"Sounds like they're giving up."

"Not really, and in a way I can't blame Nelson. He's just doing his job. We'll have regular monthly reviews and can bring in more people if we get new leads. I guess it's just disappointing. My first truly big case, and the game was called for lack of time."

"Thanks for calling," I said, thinking. "But what about the kid who supposedly drowned on spring break in Florida? I know it's a long shot, but think about it. With Klein and Juarez, the ones you called Victims B and C, you told me they focused on Jacksonville because that's where one of them lived and the other was staying. Yet their bodies were found more than a hundred miles to the north. They were much nearer Savannah, but no one searched there for them initially. Maybe it's the same thing with the kid who was supposedly in Florida on spring break. What if Juarez and Klein were up to no good, and didn't want their wives to know? Same thing could be the case with the college kid."

"You are really obsessed with that situation, aren't you?" Pete sounded very skeptical.

"Not at all. You're the one who talked about looking under every rock, or something like that. Let me make a suggestion. You've got a DNA profile on the kid, Victim A, right?"

"Yes...."

"You can rule out the need for any follow-up by comparing his DNA with that of the woman who said she was his mother."

There was a moment of silence while Pete was thinking. Then, "Wasn't her name something like Willingway or...?"

"Willingham, I believe."

"Yeah, right. I remember now. We searched the missing persons databases for a Willingham connection, but nothing came up."

"Did you ever think the kid might have a different name, like maybe his mother was divorced or widowed and she remarried and took her new husband's name?"

"No," Pete said quietly.

"Well, just send somebody to get a sample from the mother, the woman who called. If I understand it correctly, you can have her profile to compare with the victim's in a matter of days if you make it a rush job. If it doesn't match, you can discount that lead. If it does, you'll have the last of the victims identified and can throw everything you've got into chasing down what happened."

Again, Pete was silent for a moment, evidently somewhat uncomfortable at having missed a possible lead. "Now I know why you went to law school, John. You're right, and we should have done more when the lead first came in. We'll get right on it, and I promise to let you know how things are going."

This time it was eight days before Pete called me back, his voice full of excitement. "It's a hit, the college kid was the woman's son. And you were absolutely correct. She and her first husband got divorced after two kids; she remarried and took her second husband's name, Willingham. I feel like such a fool sometimes, but on this occasion a lucky fool because of you. I can't thank you enough."

"So, are you following up, or what?"

"Oh, yeah, to be sure. The big thing is that with a new lead like this, Nelson Jackson canceled the shutdown of the investigation. We're going to throw everything into it now that we have all four victims ID'ed. It's a strange mix: a college kid, two middle-aged guys associated with the construction industry, and an older widower, all murdered and their bodies concealed in a small lake miles from their home. Just doesn't make sense. We've got some of the best guys at the Bureau working with us on figuring out the problem. There's got to be a common thread here but it's eluded everyone on the team."

"How did it go with the mother?"

"About as you might expect. Deep down she realized her son was gone, but she kept holding out hope against hope that he was still alive somewhere, or that maybe he had been hit on the head and had amnesia.... She was pitiful when we gave her the news. She cried, of course, but then said they could now give him a proper burial. I think she had done most of her grieving after he originally went missing years ago."

"So, where are you going to go from here?" I asked, in some ways relieved, but still curious. The sense of relief came from what appeared to be the evident fact that nothing uncovered thus far suggested any of the Dawsons were involved in the murders and disposal of the bodies. Yes, the remains were found on property they owned, but it was rural and isolated, the ideal place to conceal corpses that a murderer did not want discovered. And sure, someone could say Nate Dawson might have killed the Wilson fellow in order to take over his job, but the more one thought about it the more ridiculous that seemed. Without assistance, I doubted that either Martha, or her daughter Jenna would have the physical strength to lug the bodies to the pond, get them out of a vehicle, place them in the boat, weigh them down with chains or concrete blocks.... The more I tried to picture them attempting to do that, the sillier it seemed.

"We'll go where the facts lead us," Pete said. "It may be that we come to a standstill again, but we know more now than we did a couple of weeks ago, and that's made a big difference. With the IDs of the victims made, sooner or later we'll find that 'magic key,' the common thread I spoke of, and it will all fall into place."

"Well, keep me abreast of what's happening...," I began, about to end the call.

"Oh, sorry, I got so carried away there telling you the good news that I forgot to fill you in on the not-so-good. You remember that I said we wanted to interview the Dawsons once again, maybe with sworn statement before a grand jury if it comes to that?

"Yeah."

"It's not gonna happen. Yesterday morning I received a call from some billboard lawyer out of Savannah who said he represented the Nathan Dawson family, and he wanted to formally advise me that they would be unavailable for any 'interrogation'—that was his word—and if we forced the matter, they had been uniformly advised to invoke their constitutional rights under the Fifth Amendment. He said he was sending us a formal letter advising us of that. I tried to be nice and non-confrontational. I honestly don't think he knew much about the details of the case. I explained in general terms what we knew and what we had found, and posed the straightforward and simple question that if his clients had nothing to do with the murders, why would they be reluctant to help us find out who committed them? He sort of backed off some of his bluster then, giving me some BS about 'consulting with my clients to reach an equitable compromise,' whatever that means. I got the impression that he had not been told the whole story."

"That's not good. It's going to make your job all the more difficult."

"You know, I've said all along that I don't think any one of them is involved, but tricks like this just make me all the more uncertain about that. From what I've seen, Nate is the headstrong type, uneducated but not stupid, probably grew up in an environment where such bluster and confrontation often replaced civilized discussion of the options."

"Sounds about right," I said. "I can't see Martha hiring an attorney, and it was Nate who got all hot when the GBI released the information on the killings. And speaking of that, did the lawyer say he was representing 'the Dawson family,' or the Dawsons individually?"

"Definitely individually. He made a point of saying he'd been retained to represent 'Nathan Dawson, Martha Dawson, and Jenna Dawson McClure.'"

CHAPTER 25

The intervention of the attorney, hired from a billboard ad or not, worried me. The Dawsons' threat to "take the Fifth" if required to submit to questioning may have simply been a ploy to tell the GBI to back off, believing they had nothing to add to the investigation and felt they were being harassed as innocent bystanders. Most Americans are not aware of the exact wording of the Amendment, one of the pillars of the Bill of Rights added to the U.S. Constitution in 1791. It states in no uncertain terms that "No person…shall be compelled in any criminal case to be a witness against himself." Paradoxically, in criminal cases, judges are required to advise juries that invoking this right cannot be seen as evidence of possible guilt. Still, the average man or woman might ask, if someone has no involvement in the crime, why would they refuse to be interviewed by the investigators? But this was now all in the past. My obsession with Jenna, as Pete Marsh had one time referred to the relationship, was over. Thinking about it now, I could not remember exactly how long it had been since I had seen her. It was past time to move on, for sure.

As a distraction, as my relationship with Jenna went sour, I had thrown myself back into the day-to-day workings of the gallery on Liberty Street. It had been both my project and passion after I was released from prison and inherited the gallery from my grandmother's estate. With the distraction of my failed relationship now fading, I once again tried to enjoy the daily hum of the business, interacting with clients, scouring local estate sales for hidden treasures. I had managed to pick up a 1940s Emil Holzhauer oil for a reasonable price, hoping to sell it for multiple times that amount to a collector. It had been on display for only two days when a stern-looking matronly woman called me over and demanded, "You do know who that artist was?"

"Yes, he was a German immigrant who was an art professor at Wesleyan College in Macon in the 1940s and early 1950s. I purchased it from an estate here in town."

"I want it," she said, tapping on the price card. "What will you sell it to me for?" That brought on a lively discussion during which I refused to lower the price and she refused to pay what was asked. Finally she said, "I have a dinner party coming up this weekend. I will pay your outrageous price if you will deliver it to my home in Macon tomorrow, take down the painting above the mantel in my parlor, and hang it there in the same place."

I smiled and said, "Give me your address and I will be there."

The painting with its golden-hued frame, now encased in layers of bubble wrap and duct tape, fit neatly and securely in the back seat of my Lincoln. Macon was a quick two-and-a-half-hour, all-interstate drive from Savannah, an easy day trip for a very profitable sale. The buyer, a lady named Mary Tutwiler, a Wesleyan graduate and originally from Mississippi, said she expected me "no later than noon." I left at eight-thirty so as to arrive in plenty of time. The Tutwilers—I later learned her husband was the retired CEO of a large manufacturing firm—lived in a neighborhood of oversized homes near Macon's premiere country club. It took me an hour to unwrap and hang the painting, and collect my check from Mr. Tutwiler, who appeared both shocked and irritated at what his wife had agreed to pay. I thanked them graciously, grabbed a bite to eat at a local McDonald's and was on my way back to Savannah shortly before one o'clock.

I'd occupied my time on the morning trip to Macon by listening to a variety of rather dull business-related podcasts. It was a beautiful afternoon as I drove back to Savannah, with a blue sky, fluffy clouds and temperatures in the seventies. I opened the Lincoln's sunroof and planned to enjoy the ride and the country air. Then Jenna crept into my thoughts. As much as I wanted to convince myself I was getting over the loss, it was a lie. I missed her, her smile, her funny little laugh, her scent in those private moments when I nuzzled her neck. I tried turning on the radio, flipping through the stations only to be bombarded with one song after another that reminded me of where we had been, or what we had done, or just her.

I had been on the road for nearly two hours when I spied the green and white sign for Exit 116 one mile ahead, with Statesboro to the north and Claxton to the south. I remembered driving back from Atlanta that Sunday afternoon after she went with me to the art show there. Had it been months or only weeks? I couldn't recall. The memories were as fresh as if it were a few days ago. Time seemed to slow, flooded with painful recollections. The second exit sign flashed into view, now one-half mile away. I could, I thought, take a slight detour through Claxton. It was not so much out of the way, and the scenery would be a break from the monotony of the expressway. At seventy miles an hour I had less than thirty seconds to make up my mind. Should I take the exit? Claxton was only about a dozen miles away. I would just ride through town, or maybe by Jenna's apartment. It was mid-afternoon and she was unlikely to be home anyway. Did wanting to do that make me a stalker? The final exit sign with its arrow pointing upwards and to the right loomed into view. At the last minute I jerked the wheel to the right and up the exit ramp, then right again on U.S. Highway 301 past a small truck stop and south toward

Claxton.

In less than twenty minutes I was on the outskirts of town, driving past the Huddle House where Jenna and I had eaten lunch the day I asked her if she would allow me to take Robert fishing. That is where this whole terrible series of events started, I thought. If she had just said "No," the bodies would still be lying peacefully on the bottom of the pond, and we would still be together. I threaded my way through Claxton's neatly laid-out blocks, slowly approaching her apartment building, a stand-alone, two-story, four-unit structure on a quiet back street. Two vehicles were parked in a small paved area in front. One of them was Jenna's. I looked at my watch. She should still be at work. Was she sick? Should I stop in and check on her? I slowed to a stop in front of the building, trying to decide if I should park and knock on her door, or be on my way. A jacked-up pickup with oversized tires and heavily tinted windows that had been parked along the street farther down the block roared to life, interrupting my thoughts as it rumbled down the street in my direction, the bearded driver leering at me as he cruised slowly past. The noise jerked me back to reality. I put my car in gear and headed home to Savannah, feeling again both stupid and foolish. It wasn't going to happen, I had to keep reminding myself.

I ate a light supper and decided to read in bed. I was just getting into a mystery novel with a great plot when my phone beeped and vibrated, signaling a text. I glanced at the bedside clock. It was nearly half past ten. Reaching over to take my phone off the charger, I tapped the green text message icon. An all-caps message filled the screen: "HEY STUPID! I TOLD YOU TO BACK OFF AND IF YOU CAN'T UNDERSTAND THAT YOU ARE GOING TO FIND OUT YOU WISH YOU HAD BUT IT IS GOING TO BE TOO LATE THEN. THIS IS NOT A JOKE."

I looked for the sender's name, but the message was unsigned. Then I recognized the phone number. It was from the same number that sent the first threatening message.

Now panicking, I quickly dialed Pete Marsh's cell, waking him from a sound sleep. "Hey, John, what's up? I was gonna call you tomorrow…."

"I got another text," I said.

Pete, evidently still half asleep, said, "Uh…, I get lots of texts every day. We all do. Why the hell are you calling me at this time of…."

"Another threat, from the same number as before."

"Oh, crap," Pete said, now awake. "You want to read it to me?"

"It can wait, but I just wanted you to know."

"Like I said, I was planning on calling you tomorrow. Something's come up in the Dawson case and I think it's something big. You need to know about it. Can you meet me at headquarters first thing in the morning?"

"Of course, but what…?"

"It's too complicated to try to go over it all on the phone. It'll wait till tomorrow. Get a good night's sleep and we'll talk then." The line went dead. Did he actually expect me to "get a good night's sleep?"

CHAPTER 26

At 9:00 a.m. the next morning I was waiting for Pete Marsh as he arrived at his temporary office in the GBI's Regional Crime Laboratory on the outskirts of Savannah. "You're an eager beaver this morning," he said, smiling.

"You left me hanging last night."

"It was late, and you woke me up. But like I said, it's big. Come on in and let's get started." He led me to a small conference room, shut the door and motioned for me to take a seat. "It's complicated, so tell me if I lose you anywhere." Pete settled in a chair and began to bring me up to date.

"Okay, to start, I have to take credit for being slow in not realizing the possibility that the son of Mrs. Willingham might not share the same last name. I have to thank you for that, and for opening up this whole case again. It seems that the victim's mother was married at an early age—about eighteen, I think—to her high school boyfriend. She had gotten pregnant, and that's why she married him, she told us. The kid was born when she was nineteen, and about a year and a half later they had a second child, another boy. The only reason for the marriage was the pregnancy, not some undying love for the father. According to her, he had no ambition, and they ended up in a single-wide in some run-down trailer park. He had a dead-end blue-collar job and it looked to her like there were no prospects of things getting any better. The one reason she stayed with him was her husband's love of the kids. He doted on them, spent a lot of time playing with them, and so on. She needed to work to make ends meet and managed to find a job as a secretary and personal assistant to the owner of a real estate holding company.

"As things would work out, she was good looking, he had plenty of money and said he wasn't happy at home. It didn't take too long for them to get 'involved,' to use her word for it. So, when she was about twenty-six, she and her trailer park hubby split, with her filing for divorce. She moved in with her boss, who by that time had also gotten a divorce. They were married within six months after that, making her the new Mrs. Willingham.

"And as things often happen in these situations, it was the kids who suffered the most. Her two sons by the first marriage loved their dad, and ended up hating their mother for breaking up the marriage. I got the impression the father sort of encouraged that. They wanted to stay with their father, and Mrs. Willingham didn't object, especially after getting pregnant by her new husband. She describes both her first husband and the two kids by him as being downright 'hostile.' Are you with me so far? Any questions?" Pete asked.

"Sounds very familiar, but go on. I'm following you," I said.

"Well, fast forward now about ten or twelve years. The older kid, William, wants to go to college. He's bright and made acceptable grades in school. His father tries to discourage that, and refuses to help out financially—I kinda think he didn't have the money anyway. So, despite their differences, William approaches his mother, who for years had felt guilty about essentially abandoning her children, and asks if she will cover his tuition and maybe help out some with other expenses. The Willinghams could easily afford it, so she agrees, in part out of remorse for her actions and in part to reestablish a bond with her son. She even agrees to give him a credit card with a limit of $500 per month for 'spending money.' Her bank would reload the card the first of every month.

"So the kid gets accepted and starts school at Georgia Southern University. The first two years go by smoothly, but despite the mother's efforts to reconnect, to rekindle a warm relationship with her son, the old resentments remain. He's friendly, but not loving and rarely visits her even though she lives not far away in Savannah. Eventually she realizes that he considers her less of a loving parent than as a source of support while he's in school. She in turn feels even more guilty, but won't admit the reality of the situation, hoping things will change. That's her private secret, she said, and let the little charade go on.

"Now here the story gets a little more interesting. Mrs. Willingham, in an effort to build and maintain a relationship with her son, would call him about once a week. Sometimes he'd answer, other times not. We don't know exactly when he went missing, or in fact any firm details. She said she invited him to join them for a few days at their mountain house in North Carolina. William said he would like to, but a buddy of his had invited him to go to Florida for spring break, which was just then coming up. She didn't ask the pal's name, and wasn't sure if William was going as he said, or just avoiding spending time with her. She said she was disappointed and he echoed the same feeling, and that was that. About a week later she gets a late-night call from a male voice—she said she couldn't tell his age—who said he and 'a bunch of guys,' including William, were staying at a motel at or near Daytona, and that they were all pretty drunk or stoned and William decided to go out to the beach by himself. They didn't think much of it, but the next morning he hadn't come back, and the caller was worried he might have drowned. She didn't get the guy's name or phone number.

"So she gets frantic, and starts calling around. She calls the police, the Daytona Beach Chamber of Commerce, and every motel in the book, but no luck. They all told her the crowds were huge, with fifteen thousand or so kids running around. There was a local investigation, but nothing more. No body was ever found so it was assumed that William may have been drunk, got carried away by a riptide and his body eaten by sharks, or something like that. The only clue she had about his being in Florida were two separate swipes on William's credit card at convenience stores in the Daytona area, one to buy gas and the other for some snacks. There was no video or any other way to prove William was the one using the card. That was it, and the card was out of cash anyway." Pete, exhausted from talking continuously, sipped on a paper cup of Starbucks coffee he had brought in with him.

"What a tale," I said. "It makes sense until you think about it. So, I guess I'd be correct in saying that there is no clear evidence he was ever in Florida, and no evidence that he was the one using the credit card."

"Right. And it's not hard to assume he never intended to go to Daytona or wherever. It was just an excuse to avoid spending time with his mother and stepfather."

"Did you interview anyone who might have known him when he was a student at Southern?"

"The cops did as part of the initial investigation of his disappearance, but came up with nothing. He lived off campus in a one-bedroom apartment above someone's garage, so he didn't have a roommate. He was not a member of any fraternity—not many close friends, it seems from reading over the old reports. But let me show you something we did find." Pete reached into his satchel and extracted a thick folder. "These are printouts of the student-run newsletter and some more items we could find in the online archives from about six months before until six months after the kid disappeared. Have a look at them." He passed a small stack of papers over to me.

The top sheet was a digital clipping from an online article on student interests. The large center photo showed a handsome young man with longish hair and a big grin holding up a small trophy. The headline read, "Winner of Local Disc Golf Tournament," with the caption, "Billy Thomson, Disc Golf Fanatic, Wins Regional Competition."

"What's 'disc golf?", I asked.

"I didn't know either. It's where players follow an outdoor course, kind of like golf but instead using frisbees instead of clubs and balls. The goal is to land your disc in the basket at the end of the course using the fewest throws."

"Oh…," I said. "So that's the kid? And his name is Billy Thomson?" It sounded familiar, but I couldn't remember why.

"Yeah," Pete said. "Billy's his nickname." He paused. "Let me show you something else that I know you'll find interesting." He shuffled through the papers and, finding a sheet displaying a large photo with a headline above and a caption below, handed it to me.

The headline read, "Spring Flings? Dancing the Night Away at Sorority Event." The photo, printed in color, presented a dancing couple, their arms entwined around one another and smiling back at the camera. The girl, dressed in a lowcut sundress with spaghetti straps, her blonde hair falling to her shoulders, looked horribly familiar. The caption below read, "Lovers tonight, but lovers forever? Only time will tell? Billy Thomson and Jenna Dawson say they plan to dance till dawn." It suddenly struck me where I had heard the name.

CHAPTER 27

I once saw an online video of an avalanche taken somewhere at a ski resort in Europe. The footage itself was recovered from the cell phone of a victim of the snowslide, a skier who, on hearing the warning sirens of an impending disaster, pulled out his phone and began videoing the increasingly massive wave of ice and snow as it thundered down the slope directly toward him. Unseen voices in the background could be heard screaming, "C'mon! Let's go! It's gonna hit us…!" For whatever reason—perhaps the skier was mesmerized by staring into the face of death—he kept filming until the last moment when the white wall overwhelmed him and the screen turned black. That was how I felt.

I should have seen the signs. I should have recognized them, but did not, or better, dismissed them as impossible. The connection between Victim D, the older man named Wilson who wore the engraved wedding band, and Nate Dawson was suggestive but seemed improbable. The collective refusal of the Dawsons to assist the investigators by their threat to cite their Fifth Amendment rights could, I reasoned, be justified by their resentment of being falsely accused. But now, with an irrefutable connection between Victim A, the Georgia Southern student, and Jenna, the woman I loved and thought I knew, I was forced to see reality, to acknowledge the avalanche of shock, disappointment and sorrow that was about to overwhelm me. I wondered if the skier, during the last seconds of his life, felt the same way. I would live, of course, but with lasting damage to my faith and belief in the innate goodness of mankind—or womankind in this case.

"Hey, John, are you still there?" I heard Pete saying.

"Uh..., yeah, sorry. I had sort of zoned out for a sec. Kind of a shock I guess, seeing Jenna like...." I didn't finish the sentence.

"I can see that," Pete said. "You had it bad for Jenna, I know, and seeing this has got to be rough. But if I can back off a little and think about this as an investigator, the Dawsons denied having any knowledge whatsoever about the bodies, or who might be the victims. Now we've got pretty solid connections between Nate and Victim D, and between Jenna and Victim A. It's obvious that these relationships by themselves don't suggest there's a reason for murder but it also suggests the fact that on at least three separate occasions, the victims were placed in their private pond, behind their private locked gate, and probably—this is speculating—using their boat unlocked by their hidden key."

"Yeah," I said again, mainly because I didn't know what else to say. "But if I remember correctly from my statistics course in college, association doesn't necessarily mean causation. Just because they were found in the Dawsons' pond doesn't mean the Dawsons killed them or placed them there."

"Absolutely true, and spoken like a great defense attorney. No one would be foolish enough to try to charge them based on such weak circumstantial evidence, but it's our job—no, I shouldn't try to include you—it's my job, to find another reasonable explanation. And that's going to be difficult at this point. We spoke before of getting a list of the people who might have had access: the church members, Jenna's friends, maybe folks at the wedding or other parties. If the Dawsons refuse to be helpful and keep trying to hide behind the Fifth, that's going to be very, very difficult. At this point, I can't see a district attorney wanting to take the case in front of a grand jury based on what we know now, but you gotta ask yourself, what are we going to find next? You probably know as well as I do that in most murder cases that make it to trial, the prosecution's case is based in large part on circumstantial evidence. Murders rarely have an audience or direct witnesses. I'm certain these don't."

"A serial killer, maybe…?" I asked.

"Possible, but not probable. I can't see it, but then I never would have rated Jenna as a suspect when we started on the case." Pete's use of Jenna's name and the word "suspect" in the same sentence stabbed at me.

"What are you planning to do?"

"I'm not sure," Pete said. "I've been brooding about it ever since we found this link. I don't consider the Dawsons dumb people, so if we present them with what we know, they may see the light and choose to work with us. If not, they will officially have to remain 'persons of interest,' to use that tired old term. That, by itself will put some pressure on them, maybe in the sense that they're not sure how much we really know and choose to cooperate. Jenna, from what I know about her, is considerably more worldly, and likely to realize the problem is not going to just go away if they refuse to try to help us. My feeling at the moment is that we should approach Jenna, lay out what we know, explain the implications of all this unchallengeable evidence and what it means for them in being thought of as innocent bystanders, or instead suspects who refuse to assist the investigators."

"Oh…," I said once again, then hesitating as I tried to process my mixed-up thoughts. "You used the word 'we.' Were you referring to your team, or were you hoping to include me?"

"You picked up on that; let me explain. Let's assume for the moment that the Dawsons are telling the complete truth as they know it. Nate Dawson, and I guess you'd have to include

Martha, are angry because their life and reputations have been disturbed because of something they knew nothing about, and have turned their anger toward the investigators mainly because there's no one else to be angry with. That might explain why they pounced on you, a sort of 'shoot the messenger' reaction. I suspect we can cajole and explain till we're blue in the face and still get nowhere. Nate doesn't seem the type to give in.

"But Jenna's different—I used the word 'worldly' a minute ago to describe her. She's intelligent and educated, she's seen more sides of life than her parents, and I suspect she more fully understands what can and probably will happen if we don't solve this case: they'll be branded as 'suspects' from now on. I can speak with her. Randy Hodges can speak with her, but she really doesn't know us and doesn't have any reason to trust that what we say, what promises we make, are legit and can be relied on. We have no personal connections; you do. She said she loved you at one time, I am sure. No matter what's happened in the meantime, I don't think that deep connection is going to disappear. She will believe and trust you if you help explain what we've found and its implications for the Dawsons' future."

"That's asking a lot, Pete. Kinda seems like I'm being used."

"Think of the alternative, John. You're not being 'used.' Assuming Jenna has no involvement, you're saving her reputation. If her input helps us crack the case, her name will be cleared and everyone wins. If it turns out she, or her parents, have some culpability, it couldn't get much worse for you than it is now. From your perspective, you would have nothing to lose."

I was silent for a long moment. "I appreciate your

reasoning, but would you give me, say, twenty-four hours to think about it."

"No problem. Do you want to meet back here tomorrow morning, or should I call you?"

"I'll call you on your cell," I said, "but I need to ask you about the text I got, the second one...."

"Oh, yeah, I almost forgot. We have been so wrapped up with these new findings that my guys haven't had a chance to follow up. We will, I promise, but I think this ID of the Thomson kid and the connection with Jenna has got to take priority. I'm still not sure that text, or the one before it, was directed at you. Sounds like a stunt some nut would pull—sending scary texts to random phone numbers. Like people who used to call 911 in the days before Caller ID, or the crazies who start forest fires to watch the fire brigades try to put them out."

"Okay," I said, somewhat uncertain and a little disappointed about Pete's dismissal of my concerns. Strictly speaking, there was no evidence at all that the two texts were related to the murder investigation, and he had lots of other, and probably more important, things on his plate.

I thought about Pete's proposal on the drive back to the gallery on Liberty Street. I had to admit he was correct, even if I was being used as a way of giving Jenna more confidence in making a decision to talk honestly with the GBI. And he was right; weighing the pros and cons of things, both Jenna and I had more to gain than to lose if she chose to cooperate. And privately, the unspoken reason, one I would deny if asked, was the opportunity to see Jeanna one more time, hoping there was still something there between us. At 9:00 a.m. the next morning, I called Pete Marsh and agreed to work with him.

CHAPTER 28

At Pete's suggestion, we met at his office to discuss which direction to take next. After a half-hour, back-and-forth conversation, I agreed to call Jenna and explain what was going on, what the investigators had discovered, and how they would like to proceed. I did not think it would be easy for any number of reasons. I wasn't sure Jenna would be willing to say more to me than a few words, and if we got beyond that point, how she would react to the discovery of the photo documenting her relationship to Billy Thomson, now known to be one of the victims. I told Pete I would call her that evening around nine, hoping Robert would be in bed if he was staying with her instead of her parents.

Back at my apartment behind the gallery, I tried to eat a light supper, but seemed to have lost my appetite, nervously glancing at the clock every few minutes as nine o'clock approached. On the hour I tapped Jenna's number into my phone. The call immediately went to voicemail, inviting me to leave a message. I touched the red icon, ending the call. Ten minutes later I tried again with the same results. At this point I realized she had most likely blocked my number, or at the least, managed to have it sent directly to voicemail if I called. Now feeling somewhat relaxed, I placed the phone on my bedside charger and picked up a book I'd been reading. I had barely finished a chapter before my phone buzzed. The screen displayed Jenna's name and number. Trying to sound relaxed, I answered with a confident, "Hello?"

"Hey," Jenna said meekly. "I saw you called, and I'm sorry I couldn't answer. I was on the phone with one of my girlfriends. She was all crying and upset, having man trouble—

they can be so frustrating. She wanted my advice. It sort of reminded me of that painting you talked about one time, The Blind Leading the Blind." She gave a little laugh.

"Yeah, Bruegel, the Dutch painter," I said, relieved that she sounded relaxed. "Are you okay?"

"I miss you, but other than that, I think I'm all right."

"I thought we had split up."

"Kinda, but I saw it more as a 'lovers spat'—isn't that the old term? You didn't call. One of us had to make the first move. After all that garbage my father and his damn lawyer sent out, I was embarrassed. I wanted to crawl under a rock. I figured you'd never speak to me again."

For a change, Jenna sounded like her old self, the person I knew. I could not detect even a shade of hostility or anger or resentment in her voice. Again I asked, "But are you really okay, or just saying that? And how is Robert? And your parents?" Better to bring them into the conversation early, I thought.

"Robert is fine. He's staying at a friend's house tonight. My mother's just all right, not at all happy with my father for the way he's been acting, especially that part about having the lawyer call the GBI and say we all were going to refuse to cooperate. Somehow my name got in there, but I didn't know about it until several days later. It upset me—no, pissed me off would be a better term—but he's my father and I depend on him for so many things. The damage was done and there wasn't much I could do. I kept thinking you would call, or if you were angry at me, call after you cooled off, but you didn't. What changed your mind?"

"Some things have come up in the investigation."

There was silence on the other end of the line, then, "Really? What sort of things? Is that why you called?"

"No, I called because I wanted to talk with you, and because I want to work with you to get this thing about the pond over and done." I deliberately avoided the words "murder" and "investigation."

"Did they—the GBI people—tell you to call me?" Jenna's tone was neutral. I could not tell if she was angry, or troubled, or simply curious.

"Not directly, no," I said, somewhat adjusting the truth. "The investigators have made two discoveries that could have a huge bearing on the direction and outcome of the case. Your father's lawyer said specifically that y'all, and by that he meant your parents and you, individually, would refuse to cooperate with the GBI, and if forced somehow to be interviewed or give testimony, you would refuse, citing the Fifth Amendment. That's how this got started, and one of the big reasons I haven't called you."

"Damn," Jenna said. "I did not know that. And the guy said he was speaking for me as well?"

"He did." Jenna said nothing. I continued, "You know the rumors that have been floating around, the ones that say the bodies were found in your family's pond so you must be connected someway...."

"I do, and they're wrong...!" Jenna interrupted, her voice high-pitched and forceful now.

"I know that, and you know that, but it's hard to convince the gossipmongers and rumor fiends out there. We need to stop this." Once again, Jenna was silent. "Look, I care about you so very much. If we're going to be together, as friends or even as more, we have to put an end to all this. As I see it, the only way that has a chance of happening is for you to talk with the people that are trying to solve these murders. I cannot make you do that, and neither can I tell you it's going to be easy." I paused, took a deep breath, and continued. "Jenna, darling, you have been through so much and you have come so far in rebuilding your life, we both know that. I don't want to see all that fall apart now. Robert needs you. I need you, and I want you to need me as well, but until and unless this mess gets straightened out, I don't think that's going to happen."

For another moment, the phone was silent. I knew Jenna was there; I could hear her breathing rapidly. Finally she said, "You're right, John. I know that, but I'm scared. I'm frightened about bringing up the past, of digging into old memories. I worry about what it might do to my parents, or Robert...."

"Be honest with me, please. Is there anything that might connect you in any way to these murders or whoever hid the bodies there in your pond?"

"No, not that I know of. I've asked myself that a thousand times. There are painful memories, for sure, my marriage for one, but there are happy memories, too. Do you remember when I asked you to take me to the pond just after the crime lab people left? Do you remember how I said it would 'never be the same'? I guess that's life. We remember the good times and try to forget the bad. I think one of my greatest and most irrational fears is digging into the past and discovering things I did not want to know."

Yet there were two new discoveries that Jenna needed to know. Pete Marsh and I both agreed that I would break the news to her, assure her of my support—trusting she had no knowledge or involvement in either situation—and get her to agree to an open discussion with the GBI. I wasn't exactly sure how to start, but began, "None of the details have been made public as yet, but the investigators have determined the identities of all four of the victims. I want to talk to you about that, and there is one other discovery that seems to be important. I don't want to discuss this over the phone…."

"Why not?" Jenna interrupted. "I want to know."

"I know you do, and I will tell you, not holding anything back. But I'd rather be with you in person, not only to answer questions or discuss anything bothering you, but also to see you in the flesh, to see how you're doing, to see your smile and hear your voice that has not been altered by miles of copper wire and fiberoptic cable." She said nothing. "When and where can we meet?"

"Would tomorrow at my place work?" Jenna asked. "I should be home by a little after five. I'll send Robert to my parents' house for the night."

"Okay," I said, then ending the call with a hasty "Til tomorrow," and "Goodbye." I didn't want to give her a chance to change her mind.

CHAPTER 29

It was nearly six by the time I arrived at Jenna's apartment. I had planned to be there earlier but got mired in the late afternoon traffic leaving Savannah. Her car was parked in its usual spot, and it appeared a couple of other residents were home for the day. The sun was getting low in the western sky now, just beginning to paint the trees with a soft red glow. Jenna answered her door on the first ring of the bell, hugging me before either of us had time to say hello. It made me remember why I had missed her so much. We chatted for a few minutes, she fixed me a cup of coffee, and we settled in her living room—me in a chair, her on the sofa—to talk.

"So tell me...," Jenna began.

"As I said yesterday, there are a couple of new discoveries that the investigators feel are important. I mentioned that they now know the identities of all four victims. Two of the bodies appeared to have been placed in the pond at the same time, but the problem is, there is no obvious connection between those two, the ones they called Victims B and C, and the other two, who they refer to as victims A and D. I hope that's not too complicated?"

Jenna, who had been listening intently, shook her head.

"Though they are guessing to be sure, the crime lab believes the bodies were dumped there over a period of several years starting about a dozen or more years ago. Since they've ID'ed them, though, they have been able to narrow the time estimates somewhat. So, let me start with the remains they call Victim D. Have you ever heard of a man named Howard Wilson?"

Jenna looked puzzled and seemed to be combing through

her memory. "The name's familiar, but I'm not sure why. Was he someone I might have known at school or in college, or even later?"

"I'm not sure you ever met him, but you might have heard his name. He worked with your father at the McKinsey wood chip mill."

"Oh, yes. I remember now. I think I was separated from Carl then, but we hadn't gotten a divorce. Robert and I were staying with my parents. It seems like he was my father's boss or supervisor or something like that. The two of us were putting a real strain on the family budget. My mother even decided to try to find a job, but things were slow at the time and no one was hiring. And then this guy, my dad called him 'Howie,' just didn't show up for work one day. He just disappeared and no one ever knew why. So they asked my dad to sub for him until he showed back up, but he never did, so they gave my dad his job on a permanent...." Jenna suddenly stopped, her eyes opened widely and her mouth agape. "Oh, my god, no! You're not saying that my father had something to do with his death, are you? I know my dad. He's a lot of blow and BS, but he wouldn't hurt a flea. No, that can't be...."

"I don't think your father had anything to do with Wilson's death, and that includes hiding the body there, but you can see what the police might think. Not to mention how the connection would sound to the general public. In the minds of many people, he'd be branded guilty until proven innocent."

Jenna buried her face in her hands. Looking up after a moment she asked, "So what do we do? What can I do?"

"Try to help the investigators find out who is responsible." I emphasized the "is."

Jenna was crying now, but nodded her head in agreement. "I will, of course."

At this point I seemed to have accomplished my goal, asking for and receiving Jenna's commitment to assisting the GBI as best she could. I considered putting my arms around her, changing the subject, telling her how much I had missed her. But there was more, and she was going to have to face that unpleasant fact. Better now than later, I reasoned.

"Jenna," I began, "there is one other thing you need to know. It's about the remains they call Victim A, the one whose body the crime lab believes was placed in the pond first. For the longest time, they couldn't get an ID even though they had a good DNA profile. And when they eventually did, it changed the whole picture of the investigation."

Jenna listened intently, dabbing at her tears. I reached in a folder I had brought with me and handed her the photo showing her arm-in-arm with Billy Thomson at the sorority dance party. For an instant she smiled, saying, "Oh, that's me in college, and the guy is..., is..., uh..., Billy Thomson. I remember...," she began, then suddenly silent as a dark shadow seemed to cross her face. She looked at me and said, "Please don't tell me he was one of the victims, please John, not Billy...."

I nodded. "The victim's DNA was a match for Billy's mother. There's no doubt at all."

Jenna covered her face in her hands and began loudly sobbing. I moved next to her on the sofa and put my arms around her. "I'm so sorry, Jenna, but someone had to break the news to you. I'm just sad it had to be me." She did not reply, still crying, her face covered by her hands.

After what seemed like an eternity, Jenna raised her head, wiped her tear-stained cheeks once more and said firmly, "We're not getting anywhere with my crying. Tell me what happened."

"The short and long answer to that is I do not know, and neither do the investigators. Billy was estranged from his mother because of a divorce…."

"I remember that," Jenna interjected.

"…and had said something about going to Florida for spring break. Supposedly he drowned in the surf and his body was never found, but clearly that story is bogus. Based on the autopsy of his remains, he appeared to have been killed by a gunshot wound to the chest, but the circumstances and exactly when and where are totally unknown. Besides his mother, you seem to be the only definite personal connection they've found, and that was random, just happens you and he were photographed together."

"I'll tell you what I remember. Carl and I had been pretty serious, but had broken up over something silly—I thought he might be seeing another girl. Then Billy came along—I forget exactly how we met, but we started going out sort of regularly. He was bright, funny and always a little outside the box. That was what made him fun, but it also made him unpredictable. Sometimes he'd call every day, then not at all for a week or two. He said all the right things, but I was never really certain how he felt about me, about our relationship. And then about halfway through the spring semester he quit calling. I thought I'd been dumped, but several months later I heard someone say he'd dropped out of school. That would have been like something he would do. Anyway, Carl kept begging me to get back together, so we did, and you know the rest of the story."

"So you had no idea where he might have been killed, or what could have happened?" I asked.

"No, of course not. It wasn't like we were just casually dating, we were a couple. We went places together, spent weekends at the beach, that sort of thing. It hurt when he ghosted me, but they didn't call it that back then. So, when it became obvious he didn't want to be with me, it was easy to go back to Carl."

"Did Billy ever meet your parents, or did you ever take him to the pond?"

"No, I learned early on not to introduce anybody I was seeing to my father. He would morph into his protective mode, grill the poor guy like he'd been—or was about to be—accused of some crime. I guess I got used to sneaking around, which is probably why I ended up like I did after Carl and I got divorced…."

"I'll ask Pete Marsh to call you sometime in the next few days so you can arrange to meet and talk. I'm not going to tell you what to do, but it might be better if you didn't tell your parents. I suspect your dad would go ballistic…."

"I guess he doesn't know about Howie Wilson."

"No, in fact besides you and me, no one outside the group working on the case knows about either Wilson or Thomson. That will change, of course, but I get the impression the GBI wants to be careful about when they make anything public and what they reveal. I just wanted you to know about this before you talked with them."

Jenna nodded again, acknowledging my words.

"Hey," I said. "Let's change the subject for a while."

CHAPTER 30

I spent the night with Jenna. Despite everything, the shock of learning the identities of two of the murder victims and their connection to both her and her father, she seemed to have regained her calm as well as her sense of humor, telling me she was sure everything would work out fine. "'And ye shall know the truth, and the truth shall make you free,' as my mother, the Bible-thumper, likes to say," Jenna told me. "On the other hand, I kinda think she'd be convinced our lying here together naked might buy us a one-way ticket to hell," she giggled. "Oh god, John, you make me so happy. I've missed you." I smiled and gave her a hug, worried not about the truth we knew, but the unknown truths we were almost certain to discover.

I left before sunup the next morning, calling Pete Marsh from my cell as I rolled through the Savannah city limits. I went over my conversation with Jenna, and her willingness to talk about what she knew, telling him it would be best if either he or Randy Hodges did the interview. She had met both of them and would probably feel more comfortable discussing painful memories. "That's great, John. Thank you," Pete replied. "Randy and I have talked at length about how to handle this with Jenna, and this time we're going to try a slightly different approach than our first interview. You were there. You saw how upset she got, and rightfully so I'd say. I honestly believe she has no direct involvement in these murders, but I have a feeling she may know more about them—or about the victims—than she realizes."

"So, what are you planning…?"

"We're still working on it. I'll let you know when we have all the details figured out. And you'll be there of course."

"For sure."

"Then we're good to go, or will be in a few days. We've gone back and gathered some more data from the families of Klein, Juarez, and Wilson, the ones we were calling Victims B, C, and D. Hope it may help jog Jenna's memories," Pete said.

"What sort of data…?" I began, but Pete cut me off.

"I'd rather not say at this point, John. We want it to be a complete surprise, just coming at things from a different tack."

"I trust you, Pete, but you've got to remember that your 'magic key' may be hidden somewhere in Jenna's memory. If you blow this chance, there may not be another."

"I realize that," Pete said, taking a deep breath and exhaling it slowly. "Give me a few more days and I'll get in touch when everything's in place." He ended the call without the usual goodbye.

A week passed before Pete called back. "I believe we're ready to go. Here's the plan. We are going to ask Jenna to give us an interview here in Savannah rather than in the sheriff's office in Claxton like before. The atmosphere there is just too intimidating and not especially comfortable for anyone. We plan to put her up in a small guest house here in town the night before, something private and comfortable. I'm presuming you'll come with her—maybe take her out to dinner and…."

"Hey, Pete, why the change?" I interrupted.

"Because, in all honesty, we want her to be as comfortable and relaxed as possible. Seems like she may be the best chance we've got, and dragging her to the sheriff's office to talk about murders that she may think we're trying to pin on her is just not the best way to go."

"Oh, okay…."

"So, as I was saying, the next day we'll come there to the guest house to interview her. It's a small bed and breakfast close to Forsyth Park, only a couple of rooms and discreet off-street parking. The kind of place where you might go to unwind, or maybe take your mistress if you don't want to be seen. We've arranged to rent the whole place for the weekend—we'll do the interview in the dining room. We were thinking you could pick her up Friday afternoon, go out that night, then do the interview on Saturday morning."

"Why not just stay at my place and...?"

"You're missing the point, John. We want this to be as low-key and comfortable as possible for Jenna. We want her to think of herself as a member of our team, someone who is trying to help us solve a crime and in the process save her family's good name. Just talking about it is going to be hard enough for her. And like I said last week, we have some new thoughts on ways to jog her memory—and before you ask again, the answer is 'No.' You'll have to wait and see. Nothing bad, I promise."

"Okay, then. Do you want me to tell Jenna that we talked and about your plans to do her interview in Savannah in a more..., more comfortable setting?"

"Yes, please do. And emphasize that we realize how stressful this process is, but the outcome will be worth it all if we can find who killed these men." He paused, then, "And John, do you think we could arrange the interview for next Saturday, with the idea that you two would come down Friday afternoon? That's four days away, short notice I know, but we want to keep up our momentum, to keep moving this ahead."

"I'll see what Jenna says. I'm free, but it will all depend on her."

Pete thanked me and ended the call. I had no objective reason to be suspicious, or leery, or harbor a sense of unease, but I could not help but wonder what new trick they had up their sleeves, and why he would not share it with me. I glanced at my watch. Jenna would still be at work, which was probably the most private place to call her. I pulled up her profile on my contact list and touched the phone icon. She answered almost immediately. "Hey, this is a pleasant surprise. You almost never call me at work."

"Yes, but I wanted to talk with you without your family around. Do you have a minute?"

"Sure, I'm in my office with the door closed doing some paperwork. Now's a good time."

"I heard from Pete Marsh. They would like to interview you this weekend if you can get away."

"I don't have anything planned, but I'll need to ask my parents to keep Robert if it's going to take too long."

"Uh…, they want to arrange for you to come to Savannah, probably on Friday for an interview Saturday morning. I get the impression we can stay over Saturday night if we want to."

"Why Savannah?"

"Privacy. Maybe more comfortable than a windowless conference room with hardback chairs and a couple of video cameras staring down at you. They've arranged a room at a small private B&B not all that far from my gallery, and suggested that I stay with you. We could go out to dinner Friday night."

Jenna seemed to hesitate, then said, "Sounds good, I think, but why are they going to all the trouble and expense?"

I wasn't exactly sure how to answer but said, "I think the best way to answer that is they realize your family's thoughts and input are vital, but your parents have stonewalled, and they want to spend more time speaking with you." I tried to choose my words carefully.

"Okay, I'll start working on it. I'll need to be sure my parents are fine with having Robert there and check to be sure I can leave here early on Friday, maybe around two," Jenna said, a possible hint of excitement in her words. It seemed all was in place. I had the rest of the week to worry about it.

I picked up Jenna at her apartment on Friday afternoon around four o'clock. She did indeed seem happy to be getting away for the weekend. I had made reservations for dinner at the Olde Pink House on Reynolds Square, a short Uber ride from the B&B and an even shorter walk from Savannah's riverfront. It was a great place for informal dining, a bit touristy, but consistently earning high praise in online reviews. Jenna had shrimp and scallops on pasta, I had an overpriced steak, and we shared a bottle of Provençal rosé. Warmed by the wine, we walked arm-in-arm down River Street, marveling at the gigantic container ships as they passed by in the reflected lights of the city. For a change, I felt calm and happy to be with Jenna. I sensed she felt the same. Would the feeling survive the next day?

CHAPTER 31

We slept well, in part because of the wine, and in part because we were tired and for a few short hours seemingly far removed from the pressures and distractions that had become so much a part of our everyday lives. The bed and breakfast was small, a nineteenth-century, two-bedroom cottage that had been exquisitely restored for its new role of entertaining guests. The sleeping areas were upstairs, while downstairs featured large living and dining rooms, a remodeled kitchen and laundry room with the latest appliances, and a quiet parking area just behind the structure, shielding our car from the street. The owner, an older woman with the demeanor of one's ideal grandmother, greeted us on arrival and said she would be there each morning to fix our breakfasts; all we'd need do is sit down and enjoy ourselves. We ordered breakfast for eight o'clock. Pete Marsh and Randy Hodges were scheduled to arrive at nine.

The aroma of coffee awakened us shortly after seven the next morning. By eight, we were seated in the dining room sipping coffee as our host brought in a huge tray with fluffy omelets, crisp bacon, and an assortment of toasts and jellies. She extracted a bottle of Prosecco from an ice bucket and poured us each a generous glass of wine. "It's Saturday," she said smiling. "Something bubbly to start your day." We smiled back, and I thanked her, wondering secretly if Pete and Randy had planned this in hopes of getting Jenna to relax. By shortly after eight-thirty, we had finished breakfast and the table was cleared. I had another cup of coffee. Jenna had a second glass of Prosecco.

A knock at the front door at nine heralded the agents' arrival. Both were dressed informally, blue jeans and a polo shirt for Randy, khakis and an open-necked shirt for Pete. Randy carried a scuffed leather satchel. After a few moments of informal conversation, Randy took a digital recorder from his bag and laid it on the table. Jenna and I sat on one side, Pete and Randy on the other. "We really appreciate your being here, Jenna," Pete began. "I hope you don't mind meeting in Savannah. It's private, and I hope the atmosphere is more relaxed than the Evans County Sheriff's Department. Let me start by saying again that you are not a suspect in these murders and so far as we know, neither are your parents, even though one of the victims was your father's supervisor. We're not here with any agenda, we just want to talk, to ask you to search your memory about things that might not seem important or connected in any way to these crimes. Do you remember how shocked you were when you realized Billy Thomson was one of the victims? You might say to yourself, 'Never in a million years would I have thought he might be,' and yet he was, as sad as that is. So, we plan to just talk back and forth today. Randy will be recording things so we can review our conversation later, and I assure you that's the only reason." Jenna had been listening intently, watching Pete's eyes as he spoke. "So, do you have any questions?"

"No," she said, her voice neutral. "Let's get started."

"Okay," Pete said, nodding at Randy.

"I believe the first thing we need to do is acknowledge the fact that all the victims' bodies were found in a pond that belonged to your family, and at least two of them had direct connections, Wilson to your father and Thomson to you," glancing at me, Randy continued, "but as John here has said, association doesn't necessarily mean causation. I totally agree with that, but we cannot ignore it. As far at the other two, Juarez and Klein, are concerned, I cannot—I should say we, the investigators, cannot—find any reason to connect them to you or your parents. So that raises the possibility that it was the killer, or perhaps killers, who had some relationship to one or more of your family. It might have been something minor, maybe someone your father took fishing, or a classmate from high school who spent an afternoon with you and a group of kids out there just having fun. And there are other, independent connections. In the case of Wilson, he worked at the same place as your dad, and you dated Billy Thomson when you were both students at Georgia Southern. We have tried and tried to put all the pieces together, but we cannot come up with anything. Maybe you can. So, that's where we want to start. I think we would like to first talk more about other potential visitors to the pond, like church groups, or your dad's buddies, and after that go over each victim individually. I know you'll probably say you don't know much about those groups, those people, but what you think might not be important could be the clue we've been searching for." He stopped, giving his words time to sink in.

Jenna appeared to be thinking, then, "That sounds reasonable."

"Good," Randy said, "First, we'll talk, then after that we have some images we want to show you, some things that might call up old memories. We already know a bit about Billy Thomson, but when you were dating did you ever take him to the pond, maybe for a picnic, or swimming or something like that?"

Jenna thought for a moment before saying, "Yes, maybe three or four times. It's been a few years and all we did in college is kind of a blur sometimes. I remember going there once with two or three other couples. It was private, we could cook hamburgers, lay out in the sun and drink beer if we wanted to—we weren't twenty-one at the time so we were sure to get hassled if we tried to do that, say, at the beach. Other than Mindy, my good friend, and the guy she was seeing at the time, I don't recall who the other couples were."

"Did you go out in the boat?"

"Yes, I remember that because Jack—I can't recall his last name—had drank several beers and had to pee, said he couldn't wait. He just stood up in the boat and did it over the side. The rest of us were on the bank and just died laughing."

Pete and Randy both grinned. Randy said, "So you had the combination to the boat lock?"

"I did, of course, and I unlocked it. No one else asked or knew—they had no reason to. And there was one other time I recall when Billy and I went with another couple. We didn't stay long and nothing much happened."

"Was there anything in those visits that might give you reason to think someone would return there on their own?"

"No, nothing. My father was—no, is—really peculiar about the combination codes for the gate and boat locks. He always stressed to me never to share them with anyone." She hesitated, thinking, then said, "But I guess someone could look at the locks after they were open and see the combinations. It's possible but I don't think it happened."

"Okay, then," Randy said. "How about the church groups, any thoughts there? And I wanted to ask if there were other groups, like maybe the local Rotary Club or Lions Club if your father was a member, or perhaps a group of your mother's friends?"

"No, definitely not there. I won't say my parents are exactly antisocial, but joining a men's club is about the last thing my dad would do, and besides her church groups, my mother is the same way. It's just not them."

"There's one other thing we haven't spoken about, and I know it's a sore subject, so let me apologize for having to bring it up. That's your wedding to Carl McClure."

I was watching Jenna as Randy spoke. She involuntarily clenched her teeth as a transient scowl flashed across her face. "Yes, I suppose we have to discuss that. There are a lot of things in your life that bring happiness or sorrow, or peace or anger, but to me, that ceremony marked the beginning of all of them rolled into one. It was among my most monumental failures. It's almost funny, I can talk about my drug addiction, or all the things I got involved in working at the strip club, but the one thing that causes the greatest sadness and embarrassment is the failure of my marriage. I truly loved Carl, and we had a wonderful child together. But then it all turned to nothingness, and along with it my hopes and dreams for what I assumed would be the rest of my life."

"Maybe you could just tell us a bit about the wedding, give us your memory as to who was there, and all that." He paused, glancing briefly at Pete Marsh, then asked, "And we need to talk more about Carl. Do you have any idea where he is now?"

"I think he's still in prison, or was anyway, the last I heard."

CHAPTER 32

For as long as I had known her, Jenna rarely, if ever, spoke of her ex. I vaguely recalled her telling me that at the time they married he was planning a career in law, but when he couldn't find a law school to accept him, he found a job in real estate sales. Overall, I didn't believe we had ever had a conversation in which she shared any details of significance. I couldn't blame her for her reticence. The marriage had been a complete failure, leaving her in an embarrassed silence and with a constant reminder in the form of her son, Robert. The mention that Carl was in prison was news to me.

Randy nodded, reaching in his satchel for a manila folder. "I know. We discovered that through a routine background check. I have summaries of his charges, convictions and his incarceration file prior to his release...," he paused, consulting the file, "about three months ago." The expression on Jenna's face changed as Randy spoke.

"I didn't know he was out," she said.

"Well, he remains on parole, of course. If I am reading this correctly, he's got close to two years on parole, then is on supervised probation for an additional five years."

"But I thought...," Jenna began.

"I know what you're going to say, and to be honest, I'm not sure why he was released. Nominally, it was for 'good behavior,' but lately we're seeing a lot of prisoners gaining early release to relieve overcrowding in the prison system. 'Good behavior' doesn't necessarily mean just that, but rather that they've been written up less often than other inmates."

"What about the...."

Randy interrupted her again, anticipating her question.

"....the protective order? It's still in place, and according to records, will stay there for the remaining two years or so of the original prison term parole, plus the five years of probation." He hesitated, studied Jenna's face for a moment, then said, "I take it they didn't notify you of his release. That was one of the requirements and conditions. They were supposed to."

Jenna nodded. "It never goes away, does it...?"

"But Carl hasn't tried to contact you, has he?" Pete Marsh asked.

"No, and I have been living in fear of the day he got free. When he was on his medicine, he did pretty well, but he hated taking it, and when he got off it...." She didn't finish the sentence.

"He knows what will happen if he violates the protective order. It's back to prison for the remainder of his original term, and the five years of probation is automatically converted to five years behind bars," Pete said.

For what seemed like an eternity, silence filled the dining room of the B&B. From the living room across the hall, the chime of a grandfather clock marked the half hour. Finally, Randy said, "Jenna, I know this is painful, but could we talk about your marriage and about your ex-husband? It may have nothing at all to do with these murder cases, we realize that, but both Pete and I feel it's something we have to explore."

Reluctantly, but in careful detail, Jenna related her story of meeting Carl while in college, of marrying him after graduation, of the unexpected but not unwanted pregnancy shortly after turning twenty-three, and of the seemingly inevitable collapse of her marriage. "I think it was the stress of failure that pushed Carl over the edge. He had been a kind and caring person, but being rejected for law school and then failing as a real estate agent seemed to change him. He had wide mood swings, up one day and down the next and finally seemed to gravitate to what the doctors later told me was a 'manic state,' with wild, totally impractical or impossible ideas about how he was going to make up for lost time with this idea or that, pouring what little money we had into these 'investments,' as he called them, and then losing everything. And with each setback, he would blame anyone but himself. He accused people of lying to him, or 'setting me up' as he called it, so they could cheat him, and blaming me for not giving him enough support even while I was trying to hold down a job and take care of a tiny baby. And then his verbal abuse began to turn physical. He would throw things at me, or slap me, or grab me in a chokehold while he yelled at me. And then one night, after Carl had downed a few beers and started hitting me, I honestly thought he might kill me, or hurt Robert, so I called 911. The police came and took him to jail. That was just the beginning of the end. Things went downhill, and when he was arrested for the third time, he was kept in the local jail and forced to see a psychiatrist. That's when he was diagnosed with 'bipolar disorder,' and put on medicine. Things seemed to improve for a while. His mood swings stabilized, but he hated the pills saying, 'They slow me down,' or 'I don't feel good when I take them,' so he would quit, and things would soon be back like before. We separated, I filed for divorce and got full custody of Robert. Carl objected, but rarely took advantage of his visitation rights. He never paid his mandated child support and eventually I lost track of him completely. I later found out he'd been sent to prison for felonious assault." Jenna paused to take a deep breath. "And all this time I've been lying to Robert about how his dad loves him...." She dabbed at her eyes with a tissue.

The room was quiet for a moment, then both Randy and Pete said almost simultaneously, "I'm sorry, Jenna."

She said nothing for a moment, then, "That's what happened and no one can change it. Let's get on with things."

The original discussion was supposed to focus on Jenna's wedding at the pond, but with the detour into the history of her ill-fated marriage, that now seemed superfluous. Randy and Pete asked about the ceremony, who attended and if she felt that people or events there might have any connection with the murders. They both seemed to agree that was unlikely, and seemed ready to move on to the next topic. It bothered me somewhat that they brought up nothing about Carl's interaction with Jenna after the divorce, or if he had been seeing his parole officer after his recent release from prison, but I kept silent, reasoning that they would come back to that aspect of things if they thought it was important.

"Okay," Randy said, "You recall when John showed you the photo of Billy Thomson you didn't have any trouble recognizing him, right?"

Jenna said she did not. He then asked if she watched the initial news conference about the murders several months prior, reminding her that they had shown some computer-generated images that could represent what the victims looked like during life. "These were based on CT scans of the remains, with an approximation of facial features of the deceased. Of course, they were guesses at best, and in spite of what we hoped for, produced no leads as to the identities of the victims." Jenna said she did not see the original news conference, and after her father called her quite enraged about what had been made public by the GBI, decided she would not make an effort to see a rerun of the event.

"Well, such things are new technology, and despite spending quite a few dollars to have the images made, they yielded nothing. Once we identified the victims, however, the situation changed. At one of our weekly conferences, someone suggested that we approach the families of Wilson, Juarez and Klein and see if they could provide us with photos of the three taken before their deaths. We would give these to the digital tech folks, and they could alter the images to show correct hair color and style, the look of the eyes and eyebrows, whether or not the victim wore a beard, that sort of thing. We tried that, and when we showed the new versions of the digitally created images to the families, everyone seemed to agree that they bore a strikingly accurate resemblance to the victims when they were alive. It may be a long shot, but we want to show these images to you, hoping that you might recognize one or more of them. You've already told us you didn't recognize the names, but sometimes you see people in certain situations and while you don't learn or can't remember their names, their appearances stay with you. And I want to be clear; we've never tried this before, so please don't hesitate to tell us if nothing you see looks familiar." Randy paused. "I know that's a bit complicated, but did I explain it clearly?"

"I believe you did," Jenna said. "If this were not such a sad and tragic thing, I would say the idea sounds fascinating."

"Good. So before we begin, and just for the record, am I clear that so far as you know, you have never seen photos, drawings, or any images of the three other victims besides Thomson? They are Howard Wilson, Miguel Juarez and Gary Klein."

"That's correct."

"Then let's get started," Randy said, taking a slim laptop computer out of his satchel. "What we have planned is an old-fashioned lineup, but done digitally. Remember in the old cop shows they used to stand the suspect on a stage with several others and ask the witness to pick him out? Same here, but because we only have images, we're going to display a group of them on a monitor and ask you if you recognize one or more out of the group. The living room across the hall there has a sixty-five inch, wall-mounted, high-res TV, a perfect place to show them. Ready?"

"I hope so," Jenna said quietly.

CHAPTER 33

We stepped across the hall and found seats on an overstuffed sofa and two equally comfortable armchairs. Placing his laptop on the coffee table and turning on the wall-mounted TV with the remote, Randy dimmed the lights. With a few clicks of the keys, the TV's screen was suddenly illuminated by the Georgia Bureau of Investigation logo casting a sinister glow about the room. For a fleeting moment I half-expected to next see the ominous face of Big Brother from the movie version of Orwell's *1984* staring back at us.

Randy spoke. "The first thing I want to show you, Jenna, are some demo photos so you can have a better feel for what you'll be looking at." With that, the screen view changed to what appeared to be large mugshot-type photos of both Randy and Pete Marsh. "Okay," he continued, "here are ordinary photos of Pete and me. Now, we had the techs take those and run them through the same process as the photos we want to show you." Next to the original images, digital versions appeared, very similar and easily recognizable, but slightly less detailed. Both the resemblance and reality of the digital images were striking. There was no doubt these were representations of the same two people, subtly different, one an actual photo and the other a "photorealistic representation," to use Randy's term.

"What we want to do next is this. We have a total of sixteen different photos for you to review. We will put them all up at once on the first screen. You'll see each one has a number in the lower right-hand corner of the image." Handing her a pad and pen, he continued, "Please study each one, and then make any notes you need. When you're satisfied you've had a good first look, you can display each of the sixteen images one by one, in order. That way you might want to rethink or refine your first impression. There is no time limit, so please don't feel rushed in any way." He looked at Jenna to see her response. She nodded affirmatively, saying nothing. "And if you want some privacy, we can easily wait in the kitchen or outside. Got it?"

Again, Jenna nodded instead of speaking. I could sense her anxiety. Randy pressed a key on the laptop. The large screen was suddenly filled with a four-by-four matrix of sixteen mug-shot-like images of men. Each was numbered, and appeared to range in age from their late thirties or early forties up to perhaps sixty. Four had beards of varying type, several had receding hairlines, and the faces of some seemed more wrinkled than those of others. All considered, it was a nondescript display of middle-aged men. Any one of these could have been a bus driver or a priest or a serial killer. The only certainty was the fact that three of them were murder victims.

Jenna looked at the screen in silence for a very long moment, then said, "Would it be too much to ask y'all to wait outside? I sense this may be an emotional rollercoaster for me. I think I might do better with a little privacy."

"Absolutely," Pete answered this time. "There are some good lounge chairs on the front porch; we'll be there when you need us." Randy quickly showed Jenna how to access the images one by one in larger format when she was ready, after which we left for the porch. Half an hour passed, then an hour. We kept our voices low so as not to disturb Jenna. Pete fetched some Cokes for us from an ice chest in his car, but generally we sat looking about the neighborhood, staring with increasing frequency at our watches.

After about an hour and a quarter, Jenna opened the front

door and invited us back in.

"I am so sorry," she began. "I know it seems I've made you sit out here forever, but I wanted to be sure of what I'm going to tell you, which means I had to dredge up all those old memories from my past I've tried so hard to forget. I may be mistaken, but I think I recognized three men from these photos. To be honest, it did not take me long to do that. Most of the time you've been sitting out on the porch I've been trying to put together people and things that happened years ago. So, where do you want to start?"

We were now sitting back in the living room with the photos of the sixteen men displayed on the large screen. "Just start wherever you'd like. Again, there's no pressure, no rush. Take as much time as you need," Pete said.

Jenna flipped open the small notepad Randy had given her. Tapping on the laptop as she had been instructed, she flipped through the images until she arrived at number 4. "This person I think I recognize because he was a regular visitor at the 'club' not all that long after I started working there. At first I had been doing just waitress work, keeping the customers happy and so on, and this was just about the time I started doing 'stage work,' and by that I mean stripping." She appeared to be studying the image for a moment. It was that of a man in his late fifties or slightly older, with a full head of gray hair. "I don't know if I ever heard his name, but the girls called him the 'Grog,' which was short for 'grabby old geezer.' The club was open from about two in the afternoon from Tuesday through Friday, then all day Saturday. We tried to close about midnight if we could get all the guys to leave. This guy usually came in around six-thirty or seven and would stay until ten or sometimes later. And for a while, he was there two or three nights a week. That's when the trouble started.

"Now, you've got to understand that in a place like this, most of the staff who work there are younger women, and most of them rely on tips for much of their income. That means cozying up to the customers, pretending you're interested in whatever BS they're spewing out, maybe suggesting you really need a good tip, that kind of thing. And if you're working as one of the strippers, there's lots more, including 'dates' with the guys if they seem okay and want to spend the money. But this guy, Grog, just took everything for granted, assumed that the girls came with the territory if he bought a drink or two. And the worse thing is that after a couple of drinks, he'd get kinda mean and demanding. I bet we called over the bouncer half a dozen times, and by then most of the girls were staying as far away from him as they could. The last time I saw him was on a Friday night, and the club was packed. He'd been drinking more than usual and was sitting at a table by himself. When I came by to ask him if he needed anything, he grabbed me and sat me down in his lap. I screamed and half the club was staring at us as the guy was pawing me and telling me how 'cute' I was or something like that until Roy, that was the bouncer, came over and told Grog to let me go and to leave the club. It was pretty obvious the guy was drunk, but after yelling and slamming his fists down once or twice, he left. And after that, no one ever saw him again."

"Did you call the cops?" Randy asked, realizing almost immediately that it was a stupid question.

Jenna looked at him with raised eyebrows and said, "About the last thing you want are the cops prowling about in a 'gentleman's club.' The little dustup with Grog and the bouncer would probably be the least of everyone's problems." Randy nodded, silently in agreement.

"So you're sure no one saw him there again?" Pete asked.

"Pretty sure. It was something we talked about for a few days, and even if he had tried to come back, the door guy wouldn't have let him in, or if he somehow did make it inside, the other girls would have told me."

"I take it you don't remember the approximate dates?"

"No, only that Robert was still a baby and I was living with my parents in Claxton at the time."

Pete and Randy looked at each other with an almost imperceptible nod. This had to be Howard Wilson. Everything fit perfectly. Pete said, "Good work. Let's move on now to the next one you believe you've recognized."

"How about the next two?" Jenna replied. "As far as I know, they were only in the club once, but it would be hard to forget what happened to them."

"Tell us about it," Randy said, leaning back in his chair and folding his arms across his chest.

CHAPTER 34

"Again, it was not too long after I moved up from being just a waitress to a stripper who sometimes waited tables. It was good for me, and for Robert, too, because the club gave me a huge jump in pay and the tips were great on top of all that. I didn't do it full time, of course. Most of what I still did was wait tables, but now the guys were all saying, 'Hey, Candi, when are you going to get back up there and dance for us?' that sort of thing. It didn't take long before I had a real following."

"Candi...?" Pete interrupted.

"That was my club name. We never used our real names—too many weirdos out there."

"Smart move."

"Well, anyway, one night these two guys—the ones in the photos—blew into the club. It was pretty evident they'd been drinking before they got there, and for sure were looking for more than a few drinks and some good food. I was waitressing that night, and I'd never seen either one of them, but they sat at one of my tables. They started hitting on me right away, and when it got too heavy it made me really angry, so before I said something I knew I would regret, I asked Tina, one of the other girls, to take over for me for a few minutes while I went back to the kitchen to cool down. I hadn't been there five minutes before I hear this commotion coming from the main dining area, yelling and then crashing of furniture. I stuck my head out and saw there was a huge brawl, the two guys going back and forth with our bouncer and doorman at first, then several other guys got into it.... It was a real mess. Finally, the two were pinned down and tied up with their hands behind their back—somebody had some cable ties—and physically carried out the front door. I went out one of the side doors to see what was going to happen in the parking lot, but not much did. Some guy who'd been in the club came out, cut the cable ties and told them he'd drive them somewhere, I think. At least he calmed them down, got them to give him their keys, and put them in a car and drove off."

"And you can say you're reasonably certain that the two drunks who got into the fight are among these images we're showing you?" Randy asked.

"About ninety-plus percent," Jenna said. "Look at numbers 9 and 11…."

Randy rapidly tapped a few keys on the computer bringing up two side-by-side images on the large display screen, one of an olive-skinned bearded man, and the other a clean-shaven dark-headed man appearing to be perhaps age forty at most. Jenna said, "The one on the left, he seemed to be doing most of the talking. He had kind of an accent and was all dressed up in a cowboy sort of outfit with these fancy pointy-toed boots and…."

"Alligator boots?" Pete asked.

"I think so, yeah," Jenna said. "How did you know?"

"Did you notice if he was wearing a fancy belt buckle, too?"

"I didn't see one, but then I didn't want to cast my gaze on that part of his body. The only reason I remember the boots was that they were waving in the air when they carried him outside."

"And the other guy," Randy asked, "Anything specific about him?"

"I think he was uncomfortable, like he'd gotten himself in a situation and couldn't figure how to get out. But that's just me guessing…."

"Those are two of the victims, Miguel Juarez is the one with the beard, and the other is Gary Klein," Pete announced. "Good ID, Jenna."

"I wouldn't have remembered them without the huge fight."

"And you said some guy helped them in their car and drove off? Did you get a look at him?"

"Not really. That was in the parking lot and the lights were not terribly bright."

"Was he a customer at the club?"

"Probably, but I don't know. Too much going on with too many people going back and forth." She hesitated, apparently trying to call up the scene from her memory. "I do remember though, he had a thick beard."

Randy, looking satisfied, said, "I think we've made some progress here. You've correctly ID'ed the three victims and in the process connected them with the club. So now...."

"There's more to it than that, and you know it," Jenna said firmly. "Sure, I've connected them with the club, but by identifying them, even if I didn't know their names and anything else about them, it's pretty obvious I've connected them with me. If you include Billy Thomson, I'm linked in some way with each of the four victims. Does that make me a suspect now? You started out today saying just the opposite. Has my being honest with you changed your minds?" She stared at Pete and Randy, waiting for an answer.

Pete spoke. "Not at all. It means you've been forthright and honest with us. You're not stupid, Jenna. You know damned well what you're doing, and with it you see how someone might make that assumption. But you could have lied. You could have said you couldn't recognize any of the faces. You were truthful, and furthermore you knew things that no one but the investigators should know, like Juarez's alligator boots. I don't think there has ever been any doubt about your truthfulness and sincerity, but you've just demonstrated your honesty. There's nothing more that needs to be said."

Jenna whispered a soft, "Thank you."

"But there is one more big issue we need to address, and that's about Carl, your ex," Pete continued. "We've checked with his parole officer and it seems he's on the straight and narrow path since he was released from prison. He's living in half of a rented duplex down near Richmond Hill, has a part-time job in a warehouse, checks in weekly, is apparently on his meds, and has been home several times when the officer made unannounced visits. Looks like he's doing his best to avoid going back behind bars. But we want to ask two things: First, has he tried in any way to contact you in the months since he's been out on parole? And second, before, when you were working at the club, did he ever show up there, or ever try to hassle you in any way?"

Jenna, now with a hard look on her face, said, "To answer your first question, no. In fact, if you recall, I was surprised—shocked, really—when you told me Carl had been paroled. He hasn't called either at home or at work. He hasn't sent word or tried to visit with Robert. I haven't seen or heard from him at all. And in case it's not obvious, that suits me just fine.

"And about your second question, yes, he did visit the club several times when I first started working there. By that time, we were divorced, of course, but I have to admit that despite all that had happened, I still had some love for him deep in my heart. And I worried about Robert growing up without a father figure. There were no delusions about us getting back together, but I wanted to let him know how much his son missed him, and...." Jenna paused and wiped a tear from her eye, then,

"That's enough of that. Yeah, he came by, had a few drinks and several times got in a fight with guys who made some wisecrack when I was on stage. Told 'em, 'That's my wife, so you better not say shit like that.' And one thing would lead to another, sometimes pushing and shoving and even a fight or two. I think he was off his meds, but I don't know. Finally, they banned him from the club. Took his photo and kept it in a book by the door. Generally, the doorman will let you in if he knows you, but for everyone else he asks for an ID. If he's not sure, he checks 'the book' and if your name's not in it, you can get in. If it is, mostly for fighting, or harassing the staff, or trying to skip without paying, you were permanently banned. So, Carl's name got in the book and so far as I know he never returned, at least not while I was working there." She paused, thinking. "That's about all I know."

We were all more than a little exhausted. Pete suggested we take a break for twenty minutes or so, have a Coke, walk around the block, or find some way to relax before we wrapped things up. As he spoke, I noticed Jenna eyeing the bottle of Prosecco still in the bucket with the melted ice, but she made no move to have another glass even though I was sure her stress level had been off the scale. Pete and Randy sat on the front porch. Jenna and I decided to stroll in the small back yard. When we were alone I said, "It's been a rough day, I know...."

"Did you expect anything else?" she asked.

"I guess not, but the pressure has all been on you. You're amazing."

"Do I have a choice? Somewhere deep inside I feared things would come to this, and they have. I feel like I'm being asked to pay for all my sins at once."

"You didn't ask for this...."

"No, but it's mine now, and the end is not in sight yet."

"Maybe not, but no matter what happens, I love you."

"Knowing that, and having Robert, is about all that keeps me going."

CHAPTER 35

Fifteen minutes later we were all back in the dining room, Pete and Randy on one side of the table, Jenna and I on the other. We all seemed at a loss for what to say, and for a few moments an awkward silence took over the room as Randy and Pete pretended to shuffle some papers from a shared folder, and Jenna and I stared out the window at the shrubbery. "Well," Pete began, "it's been a productive day, I believe. We've made some progress and...."

"That's bullshit, Pete, and you know it...," Jenna blurted out, her tone angry. "About the only thing we've done..., no..., you've done, is draw a definite connection between me and each of the murder victims. I can sit here all day and proclaim my innocence, my total lack of involvement, but will you believe me? No, of course not. It won't matter how much time passes, as my mother would say I've been branded with the mark of Cain—my future, my life, my soul, forever stained with the unspoken and unproven assumption that I somehow managed to avoid being associated with what appear to be a series of senseless murders. You'll keep digging, prying, analyzing, and hoping for that one clue...."

"That's enough, Jenna," Pete said harshly. "No, everything we've learned confirms the fact that you had no knowledge of, or involvement in, these crimes. We believe everything you've said, I promise you. But you are correct, there may be an unknown link that we haven't found at this point. Now is not the time to talk about it. We've all had a tough day, so why don't we take a break for a while? We'll rack our brains and get back to you. Your involvement in this process, all this confusion, appears more important now that it ever has been.

We don't need suspicion, we don't want to be adversaries, we are both searching for the same truths."

Jenna stared silently at Pete for a moment, then said, "I'm sorry."

"No offense taken, Jenna. I understand how you must feel." Glancing at Randy, he continued, "I believe it's best that we leave now. We'll be heading back to my office and will be there for the next several hours if you need us. Your room is reserved and prepaid for tonight as well. You'll have the place to yourselves, so stay here and try to relax." Pete and Randy gathered their papers, shook hands with us both, and left with a pleasant goodbye.

Jenna sat back down at the dining table, silently staring out the window. After a moment she said, "Would you mind handing me that wine, John?" I did. She stared at the bottle for a moment, then turned it up, drinking what was left of it. There was another moment of silence, then, "Why don't we go take a nap, John, then maybe I can get you to take me out to dinner. And I want you to know how much I love you."

Mentally exhausted, we slept for the remainder of the afternoon. As the twilight was fading, we rose and took an Uber to the riverfront area, strolling aimlessly as night fell, saying little, sometimes holding hands. After a quick meal at an upscale burger place, we returned to the B&B for the night. Not once did we mention the events of the day. "Do you think I was stupid?" Jenna finally asked as we were getting ready for bed.

"Why would I think that?" I replied. "If anything, you've probably done more today to move the investigation ahead than has been done in months."

"Remember how long I took staring at those headshot images?" I said I did. "I recognized the three men almost immediately, but most of that time I sat there weighing whether or not to play dumb, or tell the truth. And I chose the truth, maybe not fully realizing how closely it would tie me to the murders. So, like I said, was I stupid to do what I did?"

"Of course not, you were honest. I totally believed Pete when he said once again that you are not a suspect. And yeah, they're going to be looking for a link, not simply between you and the dead men, but more likely a mutual three-way connection between these victims, and you, and the murderer."

"But there's nothing there that makes sense. Yes, the Wilson guy worked with my dad, but we had never met. And the two other drunks, Juarez and Klein, the one and only time I saw them was that night in the club. The guy who gave them a lift somewhere is who the GBI should be talking to, not me. And then there's poor Billy. We dated for a while, sure, but I cannot in any way conceive of how that could lead to his murder." She said nothing for a few moments, then, "It's like a spider web, and I'm the black widow sitting there in the middle of it, luring my prey in for the kill...."

"Why don't we let it all rest for a while? I think maybe we should back off, let the dust settle and see what Pete and Randy come up with." I hesitated, trying to think of the right words. "I know that's going to be hard, but there's nothing you or I can do or say at this point. It's all up to the investigators now." She agreed, and we said nothing more about the events of the day. We slept well, and ate a leisurely breakfast on Sunday morning, declining the Prosecco this time. I dropped Jenna off at her apartment early Sunday afternoon, thinking as I drove away that she almost seemed to be returning to her old self.

That delusion on my part lasted just over twenty-four hours. Late Monday afternoon, Jenna called, obviously unhappy. "John, is this ever going to stop?" she said, her voice sounding both desperate and pleading. "Pete Marsh just called. They want to talk to me about Carl. They wouldn't say why, only that 'some things have come up,' or something like that. They want you there and asked if we could meet them tomorrow in Savannah." I said we could, and did my best to help Jenna calm down. I was somewhat surprised that neither Pete nor Randy had called me, especially if they were wanting me to accompany Jenna to the interview.

Hanging up, I called Pete, who answered immediately. Recognizing my number, he said, "Hey, John, I was just about to call you but got distracted here with another call. Did Jenna just get in touch with you?"

"Yeah, what's up? She sounded very unhappy. Said something about your wanting to talk with her about Carl."

"My mistake. I guess I should have called you first. Let me give you some background and what we're looking for. After Randy and I left you two on Saturday afternoon, we spent most of the ride back to Savannah tossing around ideas about Jenna's recognition of the three victims connected with the club, despite the evident fact that her contact with them was pretty minimal. I mean, the Wilson guy was drunk and groped her, and the other two were a couple of drunk salesmen out on the town and looking for a good time on someone else's expense account. It seems obvious that there must be a mutual connection.

"Well, we went through what seemed like a hundred possibilities, until Randy said, 'What about the ex-husband, Carl?' Looking back on things, we should have thought of that a long time ago, but didn't. As Randy reminded me, 'Seems like everyone these days has an ex somewhere. It just didn't pop into our heads early on. So, first thing this morning I call Carl's parole officer back and find out that he's gone missing.

Apparently moved out of where he was renting, hasn't shown up for his job, and hasn't contacted his parole officer. They said they had it on their list to call us, but I think that was just the old CYA, and...."

"Wasn't he supposed to be wearing an ankle monitor?" I asked.

"I said the same thing, and for whatever reason, he was not. Apparently considered low risk. I guess we'll find out...."

"So no idea at all where he is?"

"No. Supposedly he does not have a cell phone. His warehouse job was part time for three days a week so he had lots of spare time. His family denies that they've seen him. His mugshot and info is online and has been sent out, of course, but finding someone who's absconded from parole supervision is lower on the list than catching active suspects. Most of the time such guys do something stupid and get caught and sent back to prison, but he's been missing for several weeks now."

"Do you think Jenna is in any danger?"

"I can't see why she would be. And before you ask, the same would apply to their son, Robert. Carl was never especially an attentive father, so trying to snatch him sounds unlikely. They both need to be advised of what's going on, though."

"Have you told Jenna all this?"

"No. Thought it was something we should discuss in person first. That's why I wanted to meet with both of you tomorrow at my office."

CHAPTER 36

At 10:00 a.m. the next morning we were sitting in a meeting room at the GBI's regional crime lab in Savannah. For a moment, I had an eerie feeling of déjà vu, Pete and Randy on one side of a conference table, Jenna and I on the other, a vague sense of dread hanging over our heads. I'd picked up Jenna at her apartment, trying without success to allay her fears, both spoken and unvoiced, as we drove to the meeting.

"Jenna," Pete began, "I apologize for asking you to meet with us again, but we both feel we need your help. As you know and recognize, the four victims found in your family's pond could hardly be any more different. An older widowed man, two salesmen out for a night on the town, a twentyish kid you dated briefly in college. As you pointed out over this past weekend, all of them are connected with you in some way, but that doesn't imply you have any link or knowledge whatsoever about why they were killed. We ran through plenty of ideas and suggestions but the one, perhaps the only one, that kept popping back up was that all four of them were somehow after your attention, your affection, or...," he hesitated, "...or some emotional or physical connection with you. You and Billy Thomson were seriously dating for a while until he suddenly disappeared. You thought he had dumped you, but now we can reasonably assume he was murdered. As to Howie Wilson, yes, he was your father's supervisor at work and his disappearance happened to open the way for a new position and more pay for your dad, but it's a far-fetched idea that he was murdered for a promotion in a wood chip mill.

"Klein and Juarez were just plain obnoxious, drunk and hitting on you. Your then-boyfriend Billy possessed you at one time, and each of the other three wanted to, or commented on you as a female person, all in a crude and obnoxious way. It may be a stretch, but jealousy could be a motive for murder. With the exception of Billy, it wouldn't mean that you reciprocated in any way, but to someone who was or had become obsessed with you, each of the four dead men might be considered rivals, or alternatively, individuals who had insulted you. Jealousy, revenge, whatever you call it, might have led to the murders.

"And then you might ask, 'Why would anyone dump the bodies in my family's pond?' Did you ever consider that that is the single place in all the world where you publicly pledged your love, loyalty and life to one person, the man you married, your ex-husband, Carl?"

Jenna seemed stunned, silently staring at Pete as the implications of what he had just said swirled in her thoughts. Finally finding her words, she asked softly, "Are you saying that Carl is the killer? That he murdered those men because of..., because of me...?" Her voice trailed off to a near whisper as she forced out the last words.

"It's a theory, perhaps one of many, but it seems to be the only one we have come up with thus far that might explain many or even most of the unanswered questions about these crimes. We are sure all the murders occurred before Carl went to prison. We know he's capable of violence—that's what put him behind bars. And recall how he treated you. When you were married, or even before, did he ever seem overly possessive, or suspicious, or inappropriately jealous of your time or attention?"

Jenna looked down at the table, then back at Pete. "It's something I'm ashamed of, but yes, he did. Sometimes, when Robert was young and I was staying at home, I'd get a friend or sometimes a babysitter to watch him when Carl was at work so I could go shopping or have lunch with a girlfriend. If he found out, Carl would fly into a rage, accusing me of meeting a man, or something like that. And other times he would tell his boss he was sick, or had an emergency and would show up in the middle of the afternoon, trying to catch me with someone else." She looked at me and said, "It's something I've never told anyone, not even you, John. I was so ashamed and embarrassed about how he acted." I reached out and squeezed her hand.

Pete continued, "I know it's speculation, but do you think Carl would be capable of committing murder based on what you know?"

Jenna nodded without speaking, her head bowed.

"What about the pond? I can't imagine how his mind might work, but would the symbolism of the dead bodies in the very spot where you both pledged your undying love be something Carl might think of as appropriate revenge, at the same time realizing the very small probability of their being found and identified?"

Jenna looked up at Pete. "Oh, he would. That would be exactly like something he would do. Back to my religious mother who talks about an unseen god hearing our silent prayers, that's Carl, performing a symbolic act, even if he were the only one to know."

"Then we need to find him, and quickly," Randy said. "John, I would hope for the sake of both of you that Carl has fled the state, but if not you need to watch your back."

"I know," I said. "The same thoughts were running through my mind."

"Do you have a gun, a pistol?"

"I'm a convicted felon, remember?"

"Oh, yeah...," Randy said, obviously embarrassed by his verbal blunder.

"And you, Jenna. Do you have a pistol?"

"Yes, a small Glock 43 9 mm hammerless automatic I keep in my bedroom at home. I've had one ever since Carl and I separated. But I've never had to use it."

"You do know how to aim and fire, I hope?"

"My father bought it for me and gave me lessons when Carl and I split. He said he never trusted him, but thought when we decided to marry that I should be allowed to make my own mistakes."

Pete spoke. "Our goal is to solve these murders and bring the killer to justice, but I want you to know and understand there is a part of me that almost fears discovering that what we've just suggested might be the answer we've been searching for. I've been a homicide detective for many years now, and yet I'm still surprised about the depth and cruelty of human depravity—or better, just plain evil meanness. There's something inside me that keeps saying, 'I hope you are wrong on this one,' but it looks like the best theory we've come up with thus far. I understand the hurt you must be feeling...." He stopped, in a way acknowledging that words alone could never ease Jenna's pain.

"Thank you," Jenna said softly, "but let's all do what we have to do. I'll survive. I have before."

"So, where do we go from here?" I asked.

"First, as I said a moment ago, you two need to be careful," Randy said. "If Carl is in fact the person we're looking for, I suspect he realizes it would be pretty stupid for him to hang around this area knowing we're searching for him. He's probably fled the...."

"We can't afford to take that chance," I said. "We'll be

careful." Pete nodded in agreement. I turned to Jenna. "Why don't you stay here in Savannah at my place for a few days? Robert can stay with your parents. I can drive you back and forth to work every day; it's only about an hour's drive...."

"I can't do that, John," Jenna said. "It's too much and...."

"I think it's better than the alternative. I don't want you staying alone, and I believe that we'd both be safer in the apartment behind the gallery than we would at your place in Claxton. And you could see Robert every day, of course."

Pete and Randy both expressed their agreement. "It'll just be for a little while, I'd think," Pete said. "Maybe a couple of weeks at the very most."

Jenna looked at each of us, clearly reluctant. "Okay, I guess. Not much choice...." She paused. "But it seems to me that if Carl is out to hurt either one of us, he would have already made a move, or done something...."

At that moment the two threatening texts I'd received popped into my mind, but I chose to remain silent.

CHAPTER 37

Regardless of our collective fears, nothing happened. Instead of being concerned about having to stay with his grandparents, Robert was excited at the suggestion. "He must be growing up," Jenna observed, the unspoken implication being that she would miss his company more than he missed hers. "I know they don't watch his diet like I do, and there's this girl who lives just down the street…." She didn't finish the sentence. We heard nothing from the GBI other than a couple of brief calls from Pete Marsh saying they had made no progress in locating Carl McClure. The twice-daily trip between Savannah and Claxton was surprisingly pleasant as it became two extra hours Jenna and I had together, a time to chat about the day, about minor things that were happening in each of our worlds, and a myriad of other trivial and objectively meaningless things.

As we were drinking coffee together one morning, Jenna wanted to discuss the possibility of her moving back to her apartment in Claxton. "I love being with you, John, you know that. This past month has been wonderful, sharing a bed with you, waking up together each morning, our long talks, everything. But I miss Robert, too, and sometimes I think it's good to have your own 'me time,' especially if I've had as stressful day at work, or something's bothering me…."

"Sounds like marriage to me," I said.

She laughed. "Oh, you know what I mean. It's not that I don't want to be with you, but I feel like I should be spending time with my son, or taking a really long soak in my tub, or watering my houseplants, or…, well, selfish things, I guess."

"That's normal. But we need to be absolutely sure at first

that there's no word about Carl. And before you go back home to stay, I think we should get Pete and Randy's input, just to hear their thoughts." I said I'd set up a meeting with them sometime in the next few days.

Jenna and I met with Pete Marsh at his office three days later. He said the search for Carl McClure had stalled, with the investigators reporting no progress whatsoever in finding his whereabouts. "You've got to figure this wasn't something Carl just did on the spur of the moment—saw a chance to skip and took it. No, we're almost certain he's been planning it ever since he was paroled. He's not dumb—you know that, Jenna." She nodded. "He's most likely gotten a fake ID, or taken over someone's identity. We know he had a driver's license. It was necessary for him to find a job. But what we don't know is what kind of vehicle he was driving, or much of anything to point in a direction to look."

"Isn't that the job of the parole officers to keep up with such things?", Jenna asked.

"Yeah," Pete said, "but there is often a big gap between what they're supposed to do and what they actually do."

"Did you alert the cops in Claxton?" I asked.

"Oh, definitely. If McClure is somehow obsessed with you, Jenna, he'd be keeping a watch on your place. We called them right after we discovered he'd gone missing and have been checking in at least once a week. They know the location of your apartment, and say they haven't seen any sign of him, or really, anything unusual to indicate he or anyone else might be stalking you."

"So, do you think it's safe for me to move back to my apartment in Claxton?" Jenna asked. "It's not that I'm in any way unhappy being here with John, it's just that I want to see more of my son, and well…, it's just not home."

"Have you thought about staying with your parents?" Pete asked. I couldn't decide if he was actually serious.

Jenna smiled. "I'm past thirty. I have a kid. I have a life. Need I say more?"

"'Nuff said. Let me do this. I'll talk with Randy and Nelson Jackson, who's got overall responsibility for this investigation. If they're okay with the idea, it's okay with me." He paused, then, "I don't think I need to tell you, Jenna, but your ex could well prove to be a dangerous murderer. We don't want anything to happen to either you or John." Looking at me but still speaking to Jenna, he continued, "Do you think John could stay at your place for a few days, maybe a week or two."

"Sure, if he sleeps on the sofa. I want my son back, too. I miss him."

I nodded my agreement and remained silent, though it was not exactly what I would have wanted.

"Okay, I'll make some calls and get back to you."

Thanking Pete, Jenna and I left. On the way back to the gallery she was silent, apparently deep in thought, then saying, "I hope this is the right thing to do. I hope we're not making a mistake." I didn't reply.

Pete called early the next morning to say everyone had reluctantly given their permission, though they remained concerned and urged extreme caution on our part. Jenna said she would start packing after work, hoping she could be home by Saturday, two days away. I tried to remain cheerful and supportive, but a vague and inappropriate sense of abandonment and loneliness lurked in the back of my mind. I was going to miss Jenna so much. Perhaps sleeping on her sofa for a few days was better than nothing. Things had to return to normal at some point.

With my Lincoln's back seat and trunk full, we made

several trips between Savannah and Claxton, the final one on Saturday morning. "That's it," Jenna said. "Now I've got to get things rearranged back in my closet, and on my dresser, and in the bathroom cabinets...."

"Is it okay if I head back to Savannah for a while? I need to do a little catching up at the gallery. I can be back tonight by, say, sevenish if that's okay." Jenna said it was and promised to have supper ready for me when I arrived.

Everything thus far seemed typical; another pleasant day in small-town Georgia. The grass was freshly mowed, the flowers coming into bloom, and, just maybe, our lives resuming some sense of routine, whatever that was. It was just past seven when I arrived back at Jenna's apartment. The sun had not yet slipped below the horizon, but the cool evening air made it a perfect day to be outside. I parked in front of her building, taking a moment to look about. Nothing appeared amiss or out of place. Most people seemed to be home for the evening. I had been here so often over the preceding weeks that I had come to recognize the vehicles of her neighbors: the old blue Chevy belonged to the school teacher, the washed and polished Ford F-150 to the retired couple who lived upstairs above Jenna's unit. Just down the street I noted the jacked-up pickup with oversized tires parked on the curb in front of a modest house with shaggy grass. It appeared to be the same one I had seen before on the day I'd foolishly cruised through Claxton on my way back from Macon during the time when Jenna and I weren't communicating. It was the same day I had received the second of the two threatening texts, the ones Pete Marsh felt were not important.

Jenna had left the front door unlocked, so I let myself in to the wonderful aroma of fresh-baked apple pie. "I made it just for you," she said when I asked. Her small dining table was set for three. Robert, seated on the floor in front of the television, was deeply involved in a Super Mario video game. He waved and said, "Hi," before returning his attention to the figures cavorting across the screen.

Jenna and I chatted a bit as she finished preparing the meal: roast chicken breasts wrapped with thinly sliced prosciutto, accompanied by crisply roasted brussels sprouts and what she described as "my effort at apple pie" for dessert. "But no wine," she explained. "Robert is eating with us." The meal was wonderful. Robert was chatty, talking about school and glad to be home, "with my Nintendo."

By nine-thirty, the conversation had lagged. Robert was sent off to bed. Jenna hauled out a bundle of sheets, a pillow and a blanket that she said she would put on the sofa for me to sleep. "I'd give almost anything to have you in bed with me, but I don't want to give Robert the wrong impression." We sat quietly on the sofa, her head on my shoulder. I felt content.

Then the front door, which we had not bothered locking, flew open.

CHAPTER 38

A bearded man half-hurled himself into the room through the unlocked front door. A look of horror swept across Jenna's face. She seemed too terrified to speak. "Glad to see me, babe?" he asked. His right hand held a black, large-caliber automatic pistol which he waved as he spoke. "I've been keeping my eyes on you, you know?" Gesturing with the pistol, he continued, "So..., this is your boyfriend, eh? Handsome dude. I can see how you might be attracted. But you're mine, all mine. You promised that to me a long time ago, remember? Remember the 'til death do us part' bit? Well, we ain't there yet, but it may be coming soon, especially for your man friend there." He pointed the gun at me.

"Carl!" Jenna screamed.

"Well, who'd you think it would be? Santa Claus maybe? No, you're never gonna get rid of me—at least as long as you're alive. You see, I kinda thought maybe I could run off those other guys, but just as soon as I do, you seem to have another one right there. Like that piece of shit...." Carl again pointed his pistol at me. "Well, the line said 'til death do us part,' but it didn't say who was gonna die, did it? I've been sitting behind those bars for years now, and I've had a lot of time to think about it. You're coming with me, Jenna. And Robert, he's coming, too. We're gonna be a family, all of us together again. And your boyfriend there, he's got to remember that I was here first, and this is where the 'death' and 'parting' things come in—he's gotta go. So, I gotta tell you, Mr. Tool or Pool or School or whatever they call you, you gotta go, but you ain't gonna have the pleasure of the burial at sea, or maybe I should say in Jenna's papa's pond like the others did. Nope, we gonna put you in a dumpster and hope they take you to the landfill before the 'coons eat you." Carl's threatening rant was rambling and jumbled. Like Jenna, I should have been terrified, but instead I kept wondering if he was high on drugs or having a psychotic break. Or both. I decided to engage him.

"What do you need, Carl?"

He seemed surprised that I spoke, moving closer and taking a swipe at my face with the butt of his pistol. I managed to duck and avoid contact. He backed up, saying, "Oh, wait, I'm not supposed to do that now. They taught me that in prison. Anger management classes. Do not get mad, no matter what. Instead, you just lay in wait for the right time to take your revenge. We'll do that. Neater. Cleaner."

As Carl was speaking, I noticed the hallway door behind him easing open an inch or two, and Robert's face staring wide-eyed at the scene in the living room. The door then eased shut. The hall led to the two bedrooms in the back of the apartment, Jenna's on one side and Robert's on the other. Carl had not seen him. "So, where's my son?" He asked. "I bet he's in his room, maybe sound asleep." Tilting his head toward the hallway door he yelled, "Robert, hey, Robert! Your daddy's here. Come on out and visit with us here in the living room."

To my surprise, Robert yelled back calmly, "Okay, daddy, I'm coming. Just give me a minute to put on some clothes." That doesn't make sense, I thought. The last I had seen him, Robert was dressed in his pajamas.

"Okay," Carl yelled back, sitting down in an overstuffed armchair. "We'll wait." He kept the pistol trained on Jenna and me. She was now trembling. Carl started whistling an unfamiliar tune.

Several minutes passed. Carl yelled, "Robert, where are you? We need to get on the road. You and your mama and her friend Mr. Drool, all of us, are gonna take a little ride in the country. I was kinda thinking about going out to that pond where...." He stopped mid-sentence as the hall door squeaked open. Robert was standing in the doorway, still dressed in pajamas and clutching a book bag. "You said we were going somewhere so I put a few clothes in a bag to take with me."

Carl looked at Jenna and me, grinning. "That's my boy. He's smart. He knows what to do." I had an uneasy feeling that all was not as it appeared.

Still waving the pistol, Carl stood up from the chair and took a step toward where we sat on the sofa. Behind him, I saw Robert reach in the bag, extract a small automatic pistol, aim it at his father and pull the trigger twice in rapid succession. The shots were low, both striking Carl's right leg several inches above his knee. With a scream, he dropped his pistol and grabbed at his leg for an instant, then, seeing his son pointing a pistol at him, tried to leap in Robert's direction, only to have his right leg collapse under him. The bullet or bullets appeared to have fractured his right femur. He crashed to the floor, still screaming in pain. A blotch of red grew rapidly, staining his pants leg with blood. I had lunged for Carl's pistol as soon as it hit the floor and now stood over him, for a moment seriously considering using it to put him out of our misery.

"I'm bleeding, man, you gotta help me," Carl screamed at us between moans.

Jenna rushed over, took the pistol from Robert and told him to call 911. "I already have. They said they were on their way."

A sizable puddle of blood was now beginning to collect under Carl's lower thigh. I realized one of Robert's bullets had probably hit a major artery, raising the possibility of his dying of blood loss unless the flow could be stopped. Handing Carl's pistol to Jenna, I knelt over him, removed his belt, lashing it tightly around his upper leg. The blood flow became a trickle. Just at that moment the ever-closer sound of police sirens could be heard in the distance. I took the pistols from Jenna and asked her to go wait out front for the cops.

Carl continued to moan, babbling something about "not meaning to hurt anybody, just scare 'em." Robert, who had been standing by the door this entire time, walked over and looked down at his father. "Why'd you do this, son?" Carl asked. "Why'd you shoot me?"

Robert was quiet for a minute, then said, "Somebody has to be the man of the house. I guess it's my turn now." With that, he turned and walked back toward the bedrooms, saying something about changing into his day clothes.

Within minutes, the room was filled with members of the Claxton police and Evans County deputies. The bleeding from Carl's leg had stopped for the most part. An ambulance crew, accompanied by two deputies took him away. No one bothered to ask where they were going. The space, which seemingly moments before had been filled with the sounds of gunshots and yelling and screams was suddenly cloaked in a strange silence. As members of law enforcement arrived, Robert retreated to his room. He was just a kid.

As the deputies began to depart, Jenna called for Robert. After a moment, he appeared at the hallway door, fearful that he was about to be punished for what he had done. Jenna rushed over and took him in her arms. "Oh, my darling, precious Robert. You just saved our lives. I love you so much, and as long as I live I will never be able to thank you enough. I am…, no, we are so very proud of you." She held him close in silence, ignoring Robert's obvious discomfort.

After a moment, Robert spoke. "I hope you're not mad at

me...."

Jenna pulled back and said, "No, of course not. Didn't you hear me? You just saved our lives. I am very proud of you." Then, "But you found my gun. I didn't realize you knew where it was hidden. How did you know how to shoot it, and how did you know to call 911?"

"I'm not supposed to say," Robert replied. Jenna gave him a surprised look.

"What does that mean?"

"It's just you and me here now. I wanted to be able to help if something bad happened, like a burglar breaking in or that kind of thing. They taught us in school how to call 911 if there was an emergency, so I called them on your cell phone. You'd left it on the charger in your bedroom."

"But the pistol. How did you know where to find it, and how did you learn to shoot it? I love you and you did the right thing and saved our lives, but you're only ten years old...."

"I watched videos on the internet. You can learn just about anything there if you try."

CHAPTER 39

EPILOGUE

Carl McClure was evaluated at the Evans Memorial Hospital in Claxton, then quickly airlifted to the Memorial Health University Medical Center in Savannah. It appeared that the 9 mm bullets had severed his femoral artery, necessitating surgical exploration and repair if his right leg, and possibly his life, were to be saved. Because of the fracture of his femur, both orthopedic and vascular surgical teams were required, necessitating more than eight hours under anesthesia. Due to the prompt intervention, McClure was able to make a full but lengthy recovery, his six-figure medical bills funded by the State of Georgia.

McClure's initial evaluation at Evans Memorial and then at Memorial in Savannah included blood and urine drug screens which showed strongly positive results for methamphetamine. Even before receiving pain medicine, he babbled away to members of law enforcement and medical personnel about his plans to kill both Jenna and me, referring several times to the four other murdered men he had hidden in the Dawson pond. He was read his Miranda rights by an Evans County Deputy who accompanied him in the ambulance on the way to the Claxton hospital.

A Chatham County grand jury later indicted McClure on three counts of malice murder, as well as other associated felonies for the killings of Wilson, Juarez and Klein. Aside from his verbal references to the four murders, there was also circumstantial evidence against him. The local district attorney announced her plans to seek the death penalty. His court-appointed defense team advised him to seek a plea bargain, hoping for a life sentence with the possibility of parole. McClure refused, instead insisting on a trial before a jury.

At trial, McClure insisted on testifying in his own defense, a decision strongly opposed by his counsel. On examination by the prosecutor, he readily admitted returning to the "gentlemen's club" after being banned. He said he grew a beard and used a false ID to get past the doorman. He justified this by saying it was necessary to "keep an eye on Jenna," but denied any knowledge of the deaths of the three men. As to the spontaneous statements he made at the time of his arrest, both before and after being advised of his right to remain silent, he alleged that he was only talking about things he had "heard on TV." His ploy failed. It took the jury less than an hour to convict him of the three murders, and approximately the same amount of time to sentence him to death. He remains on death row while his mandated appeals wend their way through the judicial system.

Robert's tale about learning to shoot the 9 mm Glock pistol by watching internet videos turned out to be as fake as it sounded. Nate Dawson, concerned about his daughter, had purchased the pistol for her, and the same model for himself. Robert, who was spending a large amount of time with his grandparents, begged Nate to show him how to use the gun, "just in case something happens." Despite Robert's tender age, Nate was reluctantly willing to do so, but on the one condition that Robert never tell his mother. "Remember, using a gun is something you would only do in a life-or-death situation," Nate told his grandson. Robert agreed to that and made up the internet story on his own. A strange twist of fate, but it saved both of our lives.

McClure's arrest was the focus of regional and national news, with most accounts labeling him a "serial killer." Some weeks later, Pete Marsh filled me in on the subsequent winding down of the GBI's investigation. Although McClure admitted to quietly stalking Jenna since shortly after his release on parole, there was never any indication that he had considered harming her, or that he was the person who sent me the threatening texts. The jacked-up pickup truck parked down the street from Jenna's apartment belonged to a local construction worker and had no connection at all to the case. In a frighteningly humorous sidenote, Pete said that in one of the follow-up meetings shortly after McClure's arrest, an investigator commented that perhaps the GBI should publicly acknowledge Robert's bravery and decisive action that saved my and Jenna's lives. After a very short discussion, the suggestion was tabled in that it might encourage youths to consider the use of firearms to settle disputes.

When my grandmother died several years prior, I was left the art gallery, which was on the ground floor of a large, multistory, elegantly-furnished nineteenth-century house on Liberty Street in Savannah's historic district. It was the place where I had lived for many months as a child and later as a teenager, but its size and painful memories kept me from occupying it, instead choosing the tiny apartment above the old carriage house to the home's rear. With my love for Jenna, and all the changes in my life, I realized the time had come to change the place I called home. After much discussion, Jenna agreed to move into the big house with me, giving up her apartment in Claxton. She quickly found a job with the Savannah office of the firm that currently employed her. Robert was apprehensive about the move, worried about losing touch with his grandparents whom he adored, as well as friends and classmates. Both

Jenna and I are certain he will have no problem finding new friends.

As to Jenna's parents, they were less than excited about the potential move, something Jenna's mother referred to as "living in sin." Jenna pointed out to her that she was born approximately six months after the date of her parents' wedding. After that, nothing more was said.

Jenna and I are still discussing marriage, but we are not there yet.

ACKNOWLEDGMENTS

I have enjoyed writing this fourth novel in the John Wesley O'Toole mystery series, and would like to thank those who were kind enough to read the draft manuscript and offer their thoughts, suggestions and corrections. I want to thank as well the staff of Mercer University Press for their support and encouragement with this and my other recently published works. As many of the scenes and much of the action in this book take place in Savannah, Claxton and other places in south Georgia, it must be remembered that this is a work of fiction. All characters and situations are entirely products of the mind of the author and neither represent nor are based upon persons living or dead.